"No on

Stacey snapped. "My daughter comes first in my life. I would never put Emily at risk. Just who do you think you are to second-guess me—"

"Stacey, stop it," Alex said, loudly enough to break through her tirade. "I didn't say you weren't a good mother. I was just trying to help. I know you're struggling to make ends meet, and I thought that if you did want Emily to see a doctor... you might not be able to afford—so I..." Judging from the outraged expression on Stacey's face, his explanation was just making things worse.

Reacting on instinct, he slid closer to her and put his arms around her, though earlier he'd vowed to keep his distance. She gave him a shaky smile and a warm hug, then disappeared inside her house, leaving him to savor the impression that her warm, supple body had made against his....

Dear Reader,

It's February—the month of love! And what better way to celebrate St. Valentine's Day than with Silhouette Romance.

Silhouette Romance novels always reflect the magic of love in compelling stories that will make you laugh and cry and move you time and time again. This month is no exception. Our heroines find happiness with the heroes of their dreams—from the boy next door to the handsome, mysterious stranger. We guarantee their heartwarming stories of love will delight you.

February continues our WRITTEN IN THE STARS series. Each month in 1992, we're proud to present a book that focuses on the hero and his astrological sign. This month we're featuring the adventurous Aquarius man in the enchanting *The Kat's Meow* by Lydia Lee.

In the months to come, watch for Silhouette Romance books by your all-time favorites such as Diana Palmer, Suzanne Carey, Annette Broadrick, Brittany Young and many, many more. The Silhouette Romance authors and editors love to hear from readers, and we'd love to hear from *you*.

Happy Valentine's Day... and happy reading!

Valerie Susan Hayward
Senior Editor

KAREN LEABO

The Housewarming

Published by Silhouette Books New York
America's Publisher of Contemporary Romance

For my sister, Jo Lynn.

SILHOUETTE BOOKS
300 E. 42nd St., New York, N.Y. 10017

THE HOUSEWARMING

Copyright © 1992 by Karen Leabo

All rights reserved. Except for use in any review, the reproduction or utilization of this work in whole or in part in any form by any electronic, mechanical or other means, now known or hereafter invented, including xerography, photocopying and recording, or in any information storage or retrieval system, is forbidden without the permission of the publisher, Silhouette Books, 300 E. 42nd St., New York, N.Y. 10017

ISBN: 0-373-08848-5

First Silhouette Books printing February 1992

All the characters in this book have no existence outside the imagination of the author and have no relation whatsoever to anyone bearing the same name or names. They are not even distantly inspired by any individual known or unknown to the author, and all incidents are pure invention.

®: Trademark used under license and registered in the United States Patent and Trademark Office and in other countries.

Printed in the U.S.A.

Books by Karen Leabo

Silhouette Romance

Roses Have Thorns #648
Ten Days in Paradise #692
Domestic Bliss #707
Full Bloom #731
Smart Stuff #764
Runaway Bride #797
The Housewarming #848

Silhouette Desire

Close Quarters #629
Lindy and the Law #676

KAREN LEABO

credits her fourth-grade teacher with initially sparking her interest in creative writing. She was determined at an early age to have her work published. When she was in the eighth grade, she wrote a children's book and convinced her school yearbook publisher to put it into print.

Karen was born and raised in Dallas, but now lives in Kansas City, Missouri. She has worked as a magazine art director, a free-lance writer and a textbook editor, but now she keeps herself busy full-time writing about romance.

Dear readers

Here is a picture of my cat George. I wanted to draw a picture of my friend Chester but I have never seen him. You will know why when you read this story.

Love, Emily

Chapter One

Why hadn't she'd noticed how ugly the Peyton house was? Stacey Kidd wondered as she stood forlornly on the sidewalk, staring at her new home. When she'd first driven by this place a few weeks ago, her optimism must have colored her initial observations.

"It's really charming," she'd assured her mother after she had returned to Kansas City from her trip to Topeka to view her newly inherited property. "It needs a little work, that's all." *A little work?* This sucker looked like one swift kick would reduce it to rubble. What had she been thinking?

"Oh, Lord, Emily, what have we gotten ourselves into?" Stacey asked her three-year-old daughter, who stood solemnly next to her. If only she hadn't been so eager to hire the moving company and establish her independence. She should have waited until she'd had a chance to inspect the home's interior.

But the estate lawyer had promised her it was livable, she reminded herself. Even her mother, normally very cautious, had told Stacey that Chester wouldn't have bequeathed her the house if it weren't fit to live in.

Emily pointed to the house with one chubby hand. "Are ghosts in there?" she asked, smiling expectantly. Unlike her mother, Emily wasn't afraid of anything.

Stacey laughed. "It does look haunted, doesn't it?" Then she added, in her most responsible-sounding voice, "But no, no ghosts. Ghosts aren't real, you know. They're just pretend."

"Yes they are real, Mommy," Emily replied with the earnestness only a child could muster.

"Well, we'll see." Stacey took her daughter's hand and started up the walk toward the front porch. So long as Emily wasn't afraid, she supposed there was no real harm in allowing her to believe in ghosts right along with Santa Claus and the Easter Bunny.

Stacey stopped to survey the outside of the three-story house once more. She squinted and tried to picture what it might have looked like twenty years ago, but she had no recollection of it, and only a hazy memory of Chester Peyton, its previous owner. She'd been no older than Emily when she and her mother had moved away from this Victorian neighborhood to try their luck in Kansas City, and they hadn't been back.

In its heyday, this house must have been a very handsome structure, she had to concede. Built at the turn of the century, it featured a wraparound porch, lots of tall windows, and intricate, gingerbread fretwork. But the porch was supported by unsightly columns of brick, sloppily cemented into place, instead of the original carved wood. The roof was patched and repatched, the porch sagged, and the exterior was painted in at least five different colors, none of them particularly attractive.

The fact that every other house along this block had been lovingly restored made this one look even worse. If the inside was as bad as the outside, she thought, there was no way she and Emily could live here. That realization put a lump in her throat. She wanted so badly for this move to work. Here in Topeka she could start fresh, standing on her own two feet. She had relied on her mother's generosity for far too long.

The key given to her by the lawyer slid smoothly into the lock and turned easily, Stacey noted with some surprise. But when she opened the door, she was downright shocked. The place was full of furniture. Rugs covered the wood floors, pictures hung on the walls, and a pile of logs in the fireplace looked as if all it needed was a match. There were magazines on the coffee table, and a mantel clock ticked happily, its hands reflecting the correct time.

The overall effect was cozy. And creepy, she thought. Like someone still lived here. Except she knew that Chester had died months ago.

"Where're the people?" Emily asked.

"We *are* the people," Stacey answered, ruffling her daughter's straight blond hair. "This is our house. We're going to live here."

"Will Grammy live here, too?"

"No, sweetheart. She'll still live in her house in Kansas City. But she'll come visit."

"Just us'll live here?" Emily asked.

"Just you and me, kid. You'll have lots of room to play, huh?"

"Yeah, neat!" With that she broke free of Stacey's grasp and began to run around the large front room, trying out first the old blue velvet sofa, then a wingback chair, then another chair, finally landing with a plop on the faded Oriental carpet. "Play with me, Mommy."

"It's not time for play right now," Stacey answered. "It's time for exploring. Let's see what else we can find in this big old house." Once she got over the surprise, her spirits were bolstered immeasurably by the home's warm interior. It wasn't luxurious, not by a long shot, but the furniture was usable and everything looked immaculate.

She didn't recall that old Mr. Peyton's will had specifically mentioned furnishings, but apparently she'd also inherited the home's contents. She hoped so. Her own furniture, which was on its way to Topeka with the rest of her possessions, wouldn't fill up even one room of this enormous old barn.

She moved through the dining room and into the kitchen. Not modern by any means, she thought as she turned on one of the old gas stove's burners. To her amazement it ignited. The scarred sink worked, too.

The refrigerator was humming. Yes, this was definitely livable, she decided once and for all. Even if the upstairs was a mess, she and Emily could snuggle into their sleeping bags in front of the fireplace at night, if need be.

She started to leave the kitchen, but a piece of paper on the counter caught her eye. It was a message for her from Leon Pfizer, the attorney who had handled Mr. Peyton's will. She set her purse on the kitchen table, then leaned against the counter to read the note:

Ms. Kidd,

I hope everything is satisfactory. I hired a cleaning service in anticipation of your arrival, per Chester Peyton's instructions. The utilities have been turned on, with deposits paid in your name.

I'm sorry the furniture and other contents weren't removed before your arrival, but don't worry—Chester's grandson, Alex Peyton, will arrive any day to take these old things off your hands. Meanwhile, I hope this doesn't cause you any inconvenience.

There's a picture of Chester on the mantel in the living room. He especially wanted me to draw it to your attention.

Please call me if you have any questions.
—Leon Pfizer

Questions? She had at least a million and one, although right now she was too disappointed to count them. The furniture wasn't hers. It belonged to Alex Peyton.

She tried to remain cheerful. She was, after all, a homeowner, a goal that just a month ago had seemed impossibly out of reach. For the first time in her life, she was completely independent. She had a small business of her own—very small, at the moment, but already growing. And she could spend as much time with her daughter as she wanted. That was the most important thing.

Emily had taken the note from Stacey's limp hand and was scrutinizing it carefully, as if she could actually read it. After a moment she looked up. "Whas it say?"

"It says that someday soon a man is coming to take away the furniture, so don't get too attached to it."

"What?"

Stacey smiled. "It's not important, Em. Come on, let's go have a peek at our benefactor."

Emily screwed up her face. "What's a bennyfaster?"

"A benefactor," Stacey said, more slowly this time as they walked back through the dining room and into the large front room. "It's the nice man who gave us this house. His name is Chester."

"I thought his name was Benny."

Stacey smiled and shook her head. The thinking processes of her little girl never ceased to amaze her.

The photograph on the mantel, in a beautifully carved oval wood frame, wasn't at all what she'd expected. It didn't match the vague recollection she had of a lined face, thick glasses and a white beard. The man depicted here was young and vibrant, thirty years old at most. He had thick, dark hair combed back from a high forehead. His well-defined cheekbones and aquiline nose bespoke good breeding, and the wide, sensuous mouth offered just a hint of humor, as if he'd tried to remain serious for the photograph and had almost succeeded. He held a smoldering cigarette in his well-manicured hand, and an artful plume of smoke gave the portrait an extra dimension.

It was an old photograph, of course. Chester had been eighty years old when he died, but he'd once been young and—yes, sexy. She was sorry she hadn't met him fifty years ago.

"Let me see, Mommy," Emily implored.

Stacey picked up the photo and held it down at her daughter's level. "Chester Peyton," she said.

"Do I know him?"

"No. He was a very dear friend of Grammy's, though. He took care of Grammy and me for a while, when I was just a little girl and we lived down the street."

"Will he come see us?" Emily asked.

"No, sweetheart. Mr. Peyton has, um, passed away." Of course, there was no way a three-year-old could understand the concept of death.

"Like my daddy?"

"No, not exactly. Your daddy just...went away. Mr. Peyton died. That means he went to heaven." Sort of. Stacey hadn't been the most ardent churchgoer in recent years, but her mother often told Emily bedtime stories about Jesus and the saints and heaven and hell. "Going to heaven" was a handy concept Emily could probably grasp.

"With the angels?" Emily asked, obviously delighted.

Stacey sighed. "Yes, that's right."

"Can we go see him?"

"No, 'fraid not." Not for a long time, she hoped. She was about to place the portrait back on the mantel when she felt something lumpy on it. When she turned it over, she found a thick fold of paper taped to the back. Curious, she peeled off the tape, removed the paper and unfolded it.

Her hands shook uncontrollably as she read the spidery handwriting:

Dear Stacey,

I'll bet you're wondering why I wanted you to have this house. I haven't seen you since you were a wee thing, but I feel as if I know you. Your mother has kept me apprised of your circumstances over the years. In the days and weeks to come, you'll get to know me, too. And soon you'll discover I have a reason for everything I do.

Sorry about the furniture, but I had to give Alex something. He is my only flesh and blood, after all.

Yours always,
Chester

"Can I go upstairs?" Emily asked, punctuating the eerie mood that had descended over the room.

Stacey shook herself, then folded the note and stuck it in the pocket of her oversized cardigan. No reason to freak out just because she'd read a cryptic note from a dead man, one who apparently planned on hanging around. "Let's go upstairs together," she said briskly. "We have a lot more exploring to do."

"What's 'sploring?"

"Looking around. Want to pick out a bedroom of your very own?"

Emily's blue eyes sparkled as she clapped her hands gleefully. "My own room!"

They found four bedrooms and one bath on the second floor. The pipes screamed when Stacey tested the tub faucets, but they did manage to produce hot and cold water, though it was a bit rusty. So far, so good.

"Mommy! Come see my room," Emily called from down the hall. Shaking her head, Stacey followed the sound of her daughter's voice. The child was nothing if not positive of what she wanted out of life.

She'd chosen the smallest of the bedrooms. It had a dormer with a sloping ceiling and a window seat. The faded wallpaper featured tiny pink rosebuds. "Good choice," Stacey commented. She ran her hand over the smooth wood of the small double bed as Emily bounced on the quilt-covered mattress. If it wasn't an antique, it was close to it, and it had a matching nightstand. A little dresser in the corner completed the set. Emily's own white-washed pine furniture wasn't nearly as nice.

"I like the bed," Emily declared, as if reading her mother's thoughts.

"Don't like it too much, sweetheart. We can't keep it."

"Why not?"

"Because it belongs to someone else. Chester gave us the house, but not the furniture, see?"

Emily shook her head.

Stacey sighed. "Oh, well, you will soon enough." When the grandson shows up to claim his inheritance, she added silently. She wasn't looking forward to meeting this Alex. Chester's "only flesh and blood" probably wouldn't be any too friendly toward her, seeing as she inherited what should have been his house. On the other hand, he might not have any interest in the drafty old barn. As much work as it needed, it might be a liability.

"Can I have a kitten?" Emily asked suddenly.

"What? What brought that on?"

"Grammy won't live here, so can I have a kitten? Please?"

"Oh, I get it." Stacey's mother was allergic to cats, which had made a convenient excuse in the past for telling Emily she couldn't have a kitten. "I'll think about a kitten. But after we get settled in, okay?"

"Okay. Can we go to McDonald's?"

"I wish we could." A burger and a large soda sounded terrific, but macaroni and cheese sounded more economical. She had to watch every penny now. Paying the movers would take a chunk out of her savings, and so would the many things she would have to buy to set up housekeeping. Eating out was simply a luxury they couldn't afford right now.

She'd worked out her budget very carefully before committing to this move, allowing for every contingency. Provided there were no enormous emergencies, and if her modest income continued to increase as it had over the past year, her finances would stabilize within a few months.

"I want McDonald's," Emily insisted.

"You can't always get what you want, can you?" Stacey quipped. "But how about some macaroni and cheese?"

"With ketchup?"

Stacey grimaced. Emily was a precocious little girl, but she'd never be an epicure. "I guess so," she replied dubiously as they headed down the stairs. "Let's bring the suitcases in from the car."

Making her way toward the front door, Stacey noticed many details she'd missed during her first, hasty tour—the intricate molding, the art deco light fixtures, the glass doorknobs. A pair of beautifully etched French doors separated the main living room from a side parlor. All of the walls needed fresh paint and the woodwork could have used refinishing, but this house had potential, yes indeed.

She opened the front door with one hand while fishing for her car keys in the pocket of her jeans with the other. She didn't see the man standing on the front porch, reaching for the doorbell, until she'd collided with him.

They both took one step backward. "Excuse me," she said automatically, just as he murmured a like apology. Then their eyes met, and her hand flew to her mouth. "Oh, my God!"

Before she could think what she was doing she'd pulled herself and Emily back into the house and slammed the door. She leaned back against it, her heart pounding in her ears.

"Mommy?" said Emily, her childish voice filled with trepidation.

Stacey calmed herself, for Emily's sake. She forced a laugh. "Mommy's just being silly," she said. "I thought I saw a gh-ghost."

"You mean that man?"

Stacey whirled around and peered through the tiny window in the door. She must have imagined what she saw. The man was still standing out there, but through the wavy glass she couldn't make out much about his looks. Why didn't he ring the doorbell? *Because you just slammed the door in his face, dummy,* she admonished herself. He probably didn't know what to think.

She'd been unnerved by Chester Peyton's note, she'd been staring at his photograph, so the first man she saw had tended to look like him in her overvivid imagination. That *had* to be what had happened. She smoothed her hair behind her ears, took a deep breath and opened the door again—just a crack this time.

"Yes?" This time she managed to hold herself together, but damned if he didn't look like that photo of Chester. Exactly, right down to the sexy mouth with its little quirk.

He appeared at least as shaken as she felt. "I'm Alex Peyton. You obviously weren't expecting me."

She gave a huge sigh of relief. Alex Peyton, Chester's grandson. That explained the uncanny resemblance. She had to laugh at herself. "Oh, I was expecting you sooner or later. I just never imagined you'd look so much like *him*." She opened the door wider and extended her hand. "I'm Stacey Kidd."

He ignored the proffered hand, and instead studied her as if she were a side of beef hanging in the butcher's window. "So, you're Stacey. I had no idea."

"No idea about what?" she asked uncertainly, withdrawing her hand.

"No idea that Chester had such splendid taste." He smiled then, but it wasn't a pleasant smile.

Stacey drew herself up to her full five-foot-three and scowled fiercely. "Look, I'm not sure what you mean, but I don't like the tone of your voice, especially not in front of my three-year-old daughter. Lord knows you have no reason to like me..." Her voice trailed off as she realized he wasn't listening. Emily, staring up at him with none of a typical three-year-old's shyness, had captivated his attention.

"Well hi there, ladybug," he said, all of his previous animosity having vanished. "What's your name?"

Emily looked up doubtfully at her mother.

"She's not supposed to talk to strangers," Stacey explained, her voice as icy as she could make it. She still stung from the man's totally unfounded insinuation.

"But you're talking to him, Mommy," Emily reasoned.

"Emily, you're entirely too logical. Would you go get my purse? I left it in the kitchen. Maybe we'll go to McDonald's after all."

"Yea!" Emily clapped her hands together as she took off at a run.

"I'm sorry," said Alex, running nervous fingers through his longish black hair. "I shouldn't have said that in front of your little girl. But I didn't even see—"

"You ought to be sorry for saying it at all," she interrupted. "Let's just get down to business. I assume you're here to claim your furnishings."

"Not exactly. I—could I come in?"

"No." She'd answered automatically, then regretted it. He was standing too close to her, and she couldn't back away from him without closing the door in his face again. At least if she'd invited him into the living room, they could sit several feet apart.

"Look, the reason I haven't moved the furniture yet is because I'd like to make you an offer—a business offer," he added when her eyebrows flew up. "I'd like to buy the house from you."

Stacey took a moment to let that sink in. "You actually want to buy this...this monstrosity?"

"It might be a monstrosity to you, but it happens to be where I grew up." His expression changed for a moment, almost imperceptibly. But for just an instant, he looked vulnerable—sad almost.

She softened. "Look, Mr. Peyton, I'd love to sell you the house, but—"

"I'll pay a premium price for it."

"It's not a matter of price. It's your grandfather's will. The house is in trust. I won't actually own it for three years, and until then I can't sell it." She shrugged, inwardly steeling herself against Alex Peyton's certain anger. She couldn't really blame him, either.

"Why, that clever old buzzard," he said softly, more to himself than her. "He went to a lot of trouble to fix it so I can't have the house at all...unless..."

"Unless what?" Stacey asked, unconsciously opening the door a shade wider.

"Would you be open to a rental contract of some sort?"

She took a deep, steadying breath. "I never envisioned myself as a landlady."

"You wouldn't have to do anything except take in the check every month. I'd handle any repairs—"

"I'm ready, Mommy."

Both adults looked down to see Emily, whose face was half covered in coral lipstick.

"Emily, you *know* better than to get into my purse!" Stacey scolded as she pulled a tissue from her pocket and began swiping at the mess on her daughter's face.

Alex had the bad grace to snicker.

Stacey glared over her shoulder at him, wiping at the lipstick even more aggressively. "You must not have any children, or you wouldn't find this amusing in the least—" She stopped when she saw the look of pure torment that crossed his face. The expression changed just as abruptly to one of anger.

"No, I don't have any children," he said, grating the words out as if he'd chewed on them awhile first. "I don't have a wife, either, or parents, or brothers or sisters—or a grandfather, for that matter. Now it appears I don't even have my house. I hope you're satisfied."

"Me? What did I do?" Stacey squeaked.

"I wish to hell I knew. But it must have been pretty spectacular to make my grandfather disinherit me."

"But I didn't—"

"I shouldn't have come here. I'll make arrangements to move the furniture in a day or two, though God knows where I'll put it."

"I'm in no hurry," she found herself saying. "Take as long as you—" But he'd turned away from her, unhearing.

"Is he mad, Mommy?" Emily asked.

"Yes, I guess he is. Or he was." She wasn't sure. He'd sounded more defeated than angry toward the end.

She made a final inspection of her daughter's face. Overall it was still a little pinkish, but the worst of the lipstick was gone. "I'm mad, too, you know. Don't ever borrow Mommy's lipstick without asking permission."

Emily stuck her lower lip out in a well-practiced pout. "But I put it back where I found it. You said when I borrow something—"

"You should ask first. Then you should put it back when you're done. Oh, don't cry, pumpkin. Let's just forget it. It's been a long day and we're both hungry and cranky." She threw the strap of her purse over her shoulder. "Ready for hamburgers?"

"And french fries!" Emily shouted. "With ketchup."

Emily's mood bounced back to just shy of boisterous. It was always easy to fix Emily's hurts. A scraped knee was fixed with a bandage and a kiss. A nap took care of cranky tears, and the effects of a scolding lasted only until she was distracted by french fries or cookies or *Sesame Street*.

Adults were different. Stacey thought of the hurts she'd endured over the last few years, and how very long it had taken her to bounce back. Even now she constantly had to bolster her self-confidence. But she'd come a long way from those feelings of worthlessness that had once controlled her life. She was getting braver and stronger every day, and for that she was grateful.

Involuntarily she thought of Alex. Now there was a man who'd been hurt, deeply, and he had a long way to go. Maybe it took someone like her, who'd been through it, to recognize the pain. What, besides his grandfather's betrayal, had put that torment into his eyes?

Her thoughts flitted to Chester's mysterious note. "I have a reason for everything I do," he'd said to her. Why had Chester Peyton deliberately deprived his grandson of this house, which obviously meant a lot to him? She had a feeling—not an altogether comforting one—that she'd learn the answer to that question.

Chapter Two

Alex Peyton climbed into his silver Pontiac, intending to crank it up and roar off into the evening sun in a cloud of dust. But he found himself suddenly weak-feeling once he sat down. His anger departed abruptly, leaving him shaken.

He watched as the woman and her daughter climbed into a decrepit blue station wagon. Stacey Kidd was small and slender as a sappling, with a head of long, thick, straight auburn hair shot through with sunlight.

She was the embodiment of the all-American beauty. A madonna. Innocence personified.

That's what had shaken him up, the surprise of finding such an attractive, friendly young woman in his grandfather's house. A gold digger shouldn't have such a fresh face, or sincere, sky-blue eyes. As he'd peered into those incredible eyes, his world had tipped crazily for one bizarre second as he'd recognized an attraction to her. Thankfully, reality had stepped in quickly to remind him how inappropriate that was.

He sighed. Jeanne had been gone for almost five years now. She wouldn't have expected him to stay celibate forever. But to be attracted to his grandfather's floozy? No.

It seemed to take Stacey a long time to strap the little girl into her child seat in back. Then she climbed in front and started the car, which issued a cloud of black exhaust before making its noisy way down the street. The engine didn't sound good, Alex thought. He suspected the ancient wagon wasn't long for this world.

What would she do when the car gave out? Reliable transportation was essential when one had a child in tow. Suppose the little munchkin got sick and had to be rushed to the hospital?

He slammed the heel of his hand against the steering wheel, producing a welcome, distracting stab of pain. Why did he concern himself with a complete stranger's plight? Millions of mothers raised millions of children without Alex Peyton's interference.

He took a final, fond look at the homely old house before starting his own car. He could have simply sent a moving company to deal with the furniture, but he'd needed to try to regain ownership of the house. Failing that, he'd wanted to at least see the place one last time. Once he took the furnishings, it would never be the same again. Then again, since Chester was gone, nothing would ever recreate the warmth and love that had once permeated the home he remembered.

Now that he was really and truly alone, connecting to his past seemed important. Though he'd moved out on his own a long time ago, the years he'd spent in his grandfather's house represented good times, some of the happiest he could remember. He regretted not spending more time there, with Chester, during the past few years, but hell, the old man hadn't told anyone he was sick. Three weeks before he'd died, he'd appeared the picture of health. But he'd had a severe heart condition. When he'd gone, he'd gone suddenly, without so much as a goodbye.

Alex's thoughts returned to the conniving woman. She hadn't even let him inside, he thought with a surge of renewed resentment. But a few minutes later, as he ambled along back streets toward his apartment, he warned himself to be fair. Stacey Kidd didn't know him, or the situation. She'd merely been cautious by denying him entrance, which she damn sure should be as a single mother.

And just what makes you so sure she's single? The question bubbled up from his subconscious, but he answered it easily enough. If she were married, she wouldn't have hooked up with Chester.

He wanted to believe he was wrong about Stacey, but what other reason could there be for an old man to leave such a bequest to a young woman who wasn't his relative?

Chester and Stacey. It was difficult—no, impossible—to imagine. In fact, Alex was surprised that Chester hadn't introduced the woman to him. Ever since Jeanne's death, the old man had tried to thrust upon his grandson every passably attractive female he'd come across....

No, that was a ludicrous possibility. Wasn't it? His devilish grandfather couldn't possibly be playing matchmaker from the grave. Then again, Chester had known that Alex would resist an introduction to Stacey. But would the old man have died just for the sake of promoting a romance? Even for the idiosyncratic Chester, that was going a bit too far.

"Well, it won't work, Chester," Alex said aloud, shaking his head. He didn't want or need another woman in his life.

The washer and dryer would most certainly go, Stacey thought glumly as she waited for the spin cycle to finish. The movers were coming tomorrow to remove Alex's furniture, and the man was sure to claim these gleaming, almost-new appliances. At any rate, she wasn't going to argue. No matter how she looked at it, her new home was a windfall and she had no business being greedy.

The washer stopped. With the familiar, comforting background noise of Emily's solo chatter drifting from the kitchen, Stacey opened the dryer, then gave a little gasp of surprise as a small packet of papers fell out. Curious, she picked it up and untied the string, already suspecting what she'd find—another message from Chester Peyton.

Over the past couple of days, living in his house and glancing often at his picture, she'd started to get a feel for the man. Though Stacey would be one of the last persons on earth to admit a belief in ghosts or anything remotely supernatural, it was as if Chester had left a spiritual residue of some sort here.

The item on top of the packet was indeed a note from Chester, hand-written in tiny script on the back of an old recipe card. Unable to resist, she glanced first at the recipe for spaghetti sauce. It sounded promising. Then she read the note:

Dear Stacey,

By now you've surely met Alex. Handsome devil, ain't he? I hope he didn't make things unpleasant—he can do that sometimes.

I've enclosed a copy of last year's utility bills, taxes and insurance. Pretty scary, huh? If you can't make the budget balance, look to other sources of income. There's one right under your nose—or, more accurately, over your head.

Yours always,
Chester Peyton

What in the world was he talking about? she wondered as she unfolded the other papers, which included photocopies of the documents he'd mentioned. She scrutinized the utility figures for a few moments before the unpleasant reality hit her. Good gracious, January's gas bill alone was almost four hundred dollars. Add electricity, water, insurance— She scurried to her purse in the kitchen to get the calculator in her checkbook. After she'd added the numbers, she moaned aloud.

She'd never make it. Her *Baby Chatter* newsletter was operating in the black, but not *that* black.

"Whas wrong, Mommy?" Emily asked from her booster seat at the kitchen table, where she'd pushed her lunch aside in favor of a coloring book.

The cartoon mouse on the page now sported a purple complexion, Stacey noted—probably not far from the hue of her own face at the moment. "It's nothing, sweetie—just budget troubles."

"Pooey," Emily pronounced. "I hate budgets."

"You and me both." Stacey read the note again, paying closer attention this time to the part about "other sources of income." What did he mean, that she'd find one "over her head?"

She glanced through the doorway at the utility room ceiling. Nothing remarkable there. Maybe higher, on the next floor? Seeing that Emily was safely occupied, Stacey made her way upstairs, enticed by visions of a cache of jewels hidden under a floorboard. It was a ridiculous notion, she told herself. Still, through his posthumous note, Chester was trying to tell her something, trying to get her to *do* something, as he had when he'd led her to the photograph on the mantel.

When she reached the hallway above the utility room, she examined it carefully. None of the floorboards were obviously loose, but the paneling... She pushed and pulled at each of the wallpapered panels until, amazingly, one of them budged. Filled with the thrill of discovery, she slowly pulled it open on its hidden hinges, revealing a narrow stairway.

The attic, of course! With so many other rooms to explore, it hadn't even occurred to her to look for the attic. She took the flight two steps at a time, certain that this was where Chester was leading her. Another door at the top of the stairs opened into the cutest little apartment Stacey had ever seen.

She let out a tiny squeal of delight upon viewing the shiny hardwood floors and sloped ceilings, all meticulously restored. Quickly she toured the combined living room/dining room, the two small bedrooms, kitchen and bath. The walls were painted in pale shades of mint green, rose and creamy eggshell—exactly the colors she would have chosen herself.

Without even a conscious effort, she visualized her own simple furnishings filling the rooms, her pictures on the walls, her rugs on the floors.

This was the answer, of course. With one fell swoop she could prevent her own potential cash-flow crisis and inject some sense of fairness into Chester Peyton's will. It was almost too easy.

She paused on her way back down the stairs, wondering what exactly Chester had intended. He no doubt expected her to rent out the attic apartment to produce extra income. Her own plan made even more sense, she decided as she hurried back down to the kitchen phone.

When Alex's secretary had called earlier that day to tell Stacey when to expect the movers, Stacey had asked for his office number, in case any problems cropped up. She quickly dialed the number for Quincy-Peyton Advertising, bubbling over with enthusiasm for her latest idea.

Alex jumped when the phone on his desk rang. He'd been concentrating on a stack of boring sales reports for two hours, so the interruption was welcome. He stood and stretched the kinks out of his back before switching on the speaker phone and offering a pleasant greeting.

"Hello, Alex, this is Stacey Kidd."

The sound of her soft, rich voice tied his stomach into a knot. "Yes?" he answered as coolly as he dared. Stacey hadn't actually done anything to merit his rudeness—nothing he could prove, anyway—but he resented her intrusion into his life nonetheless. He'd been hoping to conclude their business without further direct contact between them.

Stacey paused before speaking again. "Look, I know we didn't get off on a very favorable note, but there's no reason we shouldn't get along."

"There's no reason we *should* get along," he countered matter-of-factly. "I doubt we'll be running into each other on a regular basis."

"Possibly not," she agreed. "Still, I've had an inspiration that concerns you, and I'd like to discuss it. Are you by chance free for dinner? I'm making spaghetti."

The invitation was issued so casually, in such a friendly manner, that Alex had to resist the urge to jump at it. Just the thought of a home-cooked meal was enough to make his mouth water. He'd lived on fast food and canned meals for far too long. But if Stacey thought to snag Chester's grandson along with his house, she was due for a big disappointment. Besides, he didn't need to be around that woman or her heart-stealing daughter. He didn't need the distraction.

"I'm making the sauce from scratch," she added when he didn't respond. "Your grandfather left me a recipe I'm dying to try out."

A recipe? Chester hadn't cooked a meal in his whole life. When Alex was growing up they'd had a housekeeper to prepare dinner. Later, the old man had taken great delight in surviving on frozen fish fillets, pizza and mint-chocolate-chip ice cream.

"Well, never mind," Stacey said hastily when Alex still didn't reply. "Maybe it wasn't such an inspired idea after all—"

"No, wait, I'll come to dinner," he said almost involuntarily. His curiosity had gotten the better of him.

"Wonderful," she said. "About seven would be convenient."

"Seven it is," he replied, forcing a little enthusiasm into his voice.

Try as he might, for the rest of the afternoon Alex could not keep his mind off the coming evening. Part of him actually looked forward to the meal. He could almost taste the garlic and oregano. But mixed with anticipation was a good dose of guilt, too. He used to love Jeanne's spaghetti dinners. Was it fair that he should enjoy Stacey's?

Then there was Stacey herself. It was hard to remain indifferent toward her. Obviously his grandfather had been charmed, and Alex was well on his way to the same fate, no matter how hard he tried to dislike her.

By the time he approached the creaky front porch of Chester's—or rather, Stacey's—house that evening, he had to keep reminding himself that she'd somehow convinced a sick old man to change his will. Until Alex figured out how exactly that had happened, he was determined not to let her work her wiles on him.

That determination was hard to hold onto, however, as soon as his hostess opened the door. Stacey greeted him with a warm if cautious smile, and he actually felt his heart lurch inside his chest. She'd pulled her long hair into a clip of some sort and curled the ends, producing a cascade of ringlets at the back of her head. Her trim body was encased in a simple white T-shirt over a denim skirt, and she was barefoot—not what he would call a calculating costume, yet it made his mouth grow dry.

Irrationally he wished he'd brought a bottle of wine.

"Right on time," Stacey said as she let him into the house. Now that she was less rattled, she could fully appreciate what a good-looking male specimen he was—tall, tanned, and probably hard as a brick wall under his navy-blue sweater. His khaki trousers delineated a muscular pair of thighs, at any rate, and she could only assume the rest of him was equally impressive.

When her eyes returned to his face, however, she saw not the pleasant mien she'd expected, but a look in his expressive hazel eyes that spoke very decisively of regret as he took in his surroundings.

"Are you thinking of your grandfather?" she asked gently.

He nodded. "It's the first time I've been here since..." He didn't have to finish the sentence.

"Were you very close?" She glanced again at the portrait on the mantel. She hadn't imagined the resemblance at all.

"He raised me," Alex said. "My father died when I was a kid and my mother—she didn't cope too well with single parenthood. Chester offered to take care of me for a few weeks until Mom could pull herself together and, well, I guess she never really did. She was—" He stopped himself. "I'm sure you're not interested."

"He must have been an extraordinarily generous man," Stacey offered.

"'Must have been?' You mean you didn't know him?"

She shook her head, causing her fall of curls to tickle her neck. "No. Not since I was three years old, anyway. I used to live just up the street, you see, and when *my* father died, Chester was very supportive. He helped Mom around the house, baby-sat with me— that's what Mom tells me, anyway. I've tried to remember him, but I can't get more than a fuzzy impression." A buzzer sounded from another room. "Oh, that's the garlic bread."

"You didn't *know* him?" Alex repeated as he followed her into the kitchen, lured by the mouthwatering scents of garlic and oregano and simmering tomatoes. He'd been half-hoping that Stacey Kidd would be a lousy cook, but those hopes were rapidly waning.

"I was shocked when I found out he had left me something so valuable in his will," she said as she removed a crusty loaf of aromatic bread from the oven.

"Mom said he was fond of me as a child, but that doesn't really explain it. Actually I was hoping you might shed some light on the situation."

"I have no idea what he had in mind," Alex said with feigned indifference. Could she be lying? No. No way. He didn't remember any such long-ago neighbors, but then, they must have moved away before he'd come to live with Chester.

He studied Stacey anew, hoping he wouldn't find her as pretty as he remembered from their first encounter. No such luck.

"Well, I know one thing," she said, lifting the lid on a large pot of what was presumably the spaghetti sauce. "It wasn't something he did randomly. He left me these notes, you see..." She scooped up a few drops of the sauce onto a wooden spoon, blew on it a moment to cool it, then tasted it. "Mmmm, this is good. Want to sample it?"

"Sure," he said automatically.

She produced a clean spoon and dipped it into the simmering sauce. "It's hot," she warned as she held it out to him.

He reached up to steady the spoon, immediately regretting the gesture as his hand collided with hers. Their eyes met for a brief instant, and his heart lurched again. Damn, he shouldn't be standing this close to her. He could smell her perfume. Quickly he put his lips to the spoon and tasted the sauce.

The moment the warm liquid hit his tongue, he recoiled as if he'd been slapped, pushing Stacey away with enough force to set her off balance and send the spoon clattering to the linoleum.

"Dammit, what are you trying to do to me?" he shouted.

She looked bewildered. "I... What's wrong? Was it too hot?"

"That's Jeanne's spaghetti sauce," he said, as if he'd just detected the taste of cyanide in the stuff.

"Who is Jeanne?"

"You don't know?" he asked skeptically.

She shook her head blankly.

"Jeanne's my wife," he finally said in a calmer voice.

"Well, for heaven's sake, why didn't you bring her with you?" She stared at him, confused and undeniably disappointed. Hadn't he said he didn't have a wife?

"I would have, but she died five years ago."

If he'd said it intending to shock her, he'd succeeded. Her hand flew to her mouth to stifle a horrified gasp. "Oh, my God," she mumbled through her fingers. "The recipe—the sauce. I had no idea." She clapped the lid on the pot and turned off the burner. "I'll fix something else. I'll make a meatloaf, that's it." She whirled around and headed for the refrigerator. "I just bought some ground beef. Or hamburgers, I could make those, too." She opened the refrigerator door and started rummaging around in the contents.

"That's not necessary," Alex said gruffly, though he recognized that at this point Stacey's distress was more acute than his own. She was embarrassed—mortified almost to the point of tears. She obviously hadn't known she was preparing Jeanne's signature sauce. He picked up the spoon off the floor and set it in the sink. "How did you get the recipe?"

She closed the fridge and sagged against it. "I told you, Chester left it for me. It was among a packet of miscellaneous papers. He'd written a note on the back. I love to try new recipes, and this one sounded good so I... I had no idea. I'm so sorry."

Alex was beginning to feel like a heel. It was just spaghetti sauce, for heaven's sake, and he'd acted as if she'd danced on Jeanne's grave. He found himself wanting to comfort Stacey, and he had to resist the urge to touch her, to smooth away all signs of anxiety from her face. "No, I overreacted. It's just that when I tasted that sauce it was like being shot back in time—"

"You don't have to explain," she said. "You have every right to be angry."

"But not at you. Chester is the one I'd like to throttle."

"Me too, now that you mention it. What on earth was he trying to do?"

Alex sighed. "I suspected it earlier, but now I'm sure. My grandfather is playing matchmaker from the grave. He was always harping at me to get a social life, start dating again. He thought I'd grieved too long."

Intrigued, Stacey asked, "I take it you didn't listen."

"No, I didn't."

"And Chester chose *me*, a complete stranger, to force on you? That doesn't make sense." Mechanically she washed the spoon and popped it into the dishwasher. Then her hands stilled. "Or maybe it does. My mother's been trying to get *me* to start dating again. Come to think of it, she didn't seem all that surprised when I inherited this house. I thought she would balk when I decided to move here, but instead she encouraged me..."

"With you owning the house and me the furniture, we *had* to meet," Alex added as he began to see the picture clearly.

Stacey shook her head. "That's so sneaky! Imagine, those two thinking they could just throw two people together and expect it to take. I'm sure they had the best intentions, but... I intend to have a serious talk with my mother about this. What about the recipe? Why did Chester leave me that?"

Alex shrugged helplessly. "Hell, I don't know. But you can be damn sure he had a reason. He was eccentric, but not senile. He always did everything for a reason."

"A reason... that's exactly the word Chester used in the first note he left. He said, 'I have a reason for everything I do.'" She shook her head again, utterly bewildered. "The whole notion is ridiculous." Then she laughed. "I mean, we probably don't have anything in common. And if either one of us were looking for a new partner, we wouldn't need to subscribe to Chester and Betty's Dating Service, right?"

Alex nodded, though it was disappointing to hear himself so lightly dismissed as a potential partner. Not that he'd even for a moment consider her, either, he reminded himself.

"Look," he said, "why don't we just go out to dinner?"

She shook her head. "It's a nice thought, but Emily's already in bed and I don't even know any babysitters yet."

Emily. He was surprised to realize he hadn't even wondered where she was. He'd been looking forward to seeing the little charmer again, but Stacey's presence had distracted him too thoroughly. "Well, maybe another time," he said. "I suppose it makes more sense to give up on this evening, given the way it's gone so far."

He fought against a stab of disappointment as they said awkward goodbyes at the front door. He was almost outside when he remembered the reason he'd come over in the first place.

"Wait a minute, didn't you want to discuss something with me?"

She waved her hand in a gesture of dismissal. "It was a dumb idea. Something inspired by Chester, as a matter of fact, so I probably shouldn't even mention it. I'll find another way to deal with the problem."

"What problem?" He closed the door again and leaned against it, facing her.

"It's just that I didn't dream the upkeep on this house would be so expensive. There's no way I can handle it on my current income. I guess Chester knew that, because he hinted that I should rent out the apartment upstairs."

"And you thought I'd want to rent it?" Alex didn't know whether to feel amused or insulted that she'd just suggested he live in the servants' quarters.

"No, that's not it at all," she said quickly. "I thought Emily and I could move up there. To tell you the truth, this house seems awfully big to me. It makes me nervous. And the apartment is just the right size for us—my furniture would fit beautifully."

"And I could have the rest of the house?" he asked, lifting a dubious eyebrow.

"Right. All I'd need is enough rent to offset the utilities. If you moved in you could leave your furnishings where they are, you see," she continued, her words rushed, "and the other day you even suggested a rental agreement of some type, and I thought—" She took a deep breath. "Well, like I said, it was a dumb idea."

It was a terrible idea, Alex thought. He couldn't share a house with her, even if they would be in completely separate living quarters. The situation would be much too unsettling. He was used to solitude, peace and quiet. No, it would never work. He told her so.

"That's what I thought," she said with a resigned sigh. "Well, I'm sure I can find someone to rent the house, even unfurnished."

He didn't mention the next thought that occurred to him—that any qualified tenant would take one look at the home's exterior and drive off without ever seeing the inside.

There didn't seem to be much left to say. Alex bid her goodbye one last time and made his escape, intending to go home, open a can of soup and forget this disturbing business as soon as possible.

Unfortunately he couldn't forget it. He kept thinking of Stacey's predicament and wondering what sort of renter she'd find. No telling what sordid influences she'd be exposing her daughter to.

By morning he knew what he had to do. It wouldn't be an ideal situation, but Stacey needed someone to share the expenses of that monstrosity, and he was the logical choice. By renting from her, he wouldn't have to move Chester's furniture into storage.

He'd been thinking of getting rid of this apartment, anyway. The place had felt empty for too long.

By the time he'd showered and shaved, he'd rationalized his change of mind a hundred different ways. Before he'd even gotten dressed, he picked up the cordless phone and dialed Stacey's number.

Stacey was so surprised to hear from Alex again that she didn't catch his first few words.

"...and so I've reconsidered," he explained in a reasonable voice. "Your idea makes a lot of sense."

Her heart raced as her hand clenched the telephone receiver. He'd changed his mind? Then it finally hit her. Good Lord, he actually wanted to move into this house. When just the sound of his voice caused her to glow like a Christmas tree, how could she cope with him on a day-to-day basis? She never should have mentioned it last night.

"...so you can see it's the most advantageous plan for both of us." He paused. "Right?"

"I, uh..." Her mind raced as fast as her heart. Why was he doing this? By the tone of his voice, he was no more thrilled at the prospect of sharing her roof than she was. In fact, he sounded almost resigned, as if he knew he had to swallow a bad-tasting medicine to cure whatever ailed him.

"It could work, I guess," she agreed reluctantly, because there seemed nothing else sensible to say.

He jumped on her cautious acquiescence, and before she knew what was happening, they were negotiating rent and move-in dates. And just when she thought she might jump in and call a halt to the insanity, he offered to help her move her things into the attic apartment. Faced with such an unselfish gesture, she couldn't find it in herself to thwart him.

After she'd hung up the phone, she wondered if an asphalt road felt the same way right after the steamroller passes over it.

Even as her rational mind pondered how she would cope with this startling change of circumstances, she felt a little thrill at the prospect. Alex Peyton, with his quicksilver emotions and hair-trigger temper, was not an easy man to deal with. Then again, she'd always enjoyed a challenge. As that thought crossed her mind, she glanced at the photo of Chester on the mantel. If she didn't know better, she'd have sworn he was grinning at her.

Chapter Three

Stacey absently wound the phone cord around her finger as she leaned against the kitchen counter. "You and Chester planned this whole thing out, didn't you?" she asked her mother, though she didn't put much bite in the accusation. Betty Kidd wanted only the best for her daughter; if she'd entered into a conspiracy with Chester to play matchmaker, she'd done it with the noblest of intentions.

"Stacey, dear, whatever are you talking about?" Betty asked innocently.

"Me and this house, Alex and the furniture. Lonely, single Mom meets lonely widower—"

"Who is Alex?"

Stacey had to smile at her mother's evasiveness. "Alex Peyton, Chester's grandson," she explained patiently. "He's terrific-looking, I'll grant you that, and not what you'd call dull, either, but we're not at all compatible."

"Chester had a grandson?"

"Oh, Mom, you're impossible! Look, I know you'd like for me to fall in love and get married and find a new father for Emily, but Alex isn't the guy. Oh, and by the way, the house is ugly as sin. I didn't mention that when I called you the other day, because I didn't want to worry you."

"Oh, dear. I know it's been years since I saw the house, but it used to be very nice..."

Betty sounded so genuinely distressed that Stacey was immediately contrite for causing her to worry. "But it's livable, very livable," she said quickly. "Just the outside is ugly. Anyway, I wanted to give you a progress report. Emily and I are moving into the attic apartment. I'm renting the rest of the house to Alex. Your plan worked at least that far."

"What plan?"

Stacey laughed. "I love you, Mom. How many mothers would go to such lengths to introduce their daughter to a nice man?"

"He is nice, then?"

Stacey heard a car pull up out front. "Gotta go, Mom, Alex is here. I'll give your love to Em. We miss you."

"I miss you too, sweetheart," Betty replied vaguely before they hung up. She sounded just bewildered enough that Stacey wondered if she and Alex weren't wrong. Maybe Chester hadn't had matchmaking in mind, but something altogether different. And maybe her mother was as much in the dark as they were.

Her breath caught in her throat when she saw Alex get out of his car. He wore a snug T-shirt with a "Buddy's Gym" logo on the front and a pair of faded jeans that had been washed and rewashed until they fit almost too well. The bright morning sun caught his dark hair in a halo and cast his face in dramatic relief. He was just about the most attractive man she'd ever seen, even as he scowled up at the house. She hoped she wasn't the one to cause that dark expression, she thought as she made her way out the door and down the walk toward the street.

"That's all you brought?" She stared in amazement at the two suitcases and three boxes stashed in Alex's car, parked at the curb.

He shrugged. "I travel light." He'd brought only his clothes and a few personal things, and boxed up the rest for storage. If he remembered correctly, Chester's house was stocked with everything a tenant could possibly need.

Once he'd decided to rent from Stacey, it hadn't taken him long to get the ball rolling. His landlord hadn't blinked an eye when Alex announced he was breaking his lease. It seemed there was a waiting list for Topeka's most elegant apartment complex. Now, on this bright, warm April morning, he was moving—and still debating with himself the wisdom of his decision.

"Well, I can see it won't take much to get you settled in," Stacey said cheerfully as she reached into the trunk and pulled a box into her arms.

"Wait, that one's probably too heavy—" Alex started to object, but she was already striding toward the house with the box propped against one shapely hip. He grabbed the two suitcases and followed her.

"I had a second set of keys made," she said as she strolled through the open front door. "Unfortunately, except for the fire escape, the only access to the attic is through the house. I don't plan to be coming and going a lot, and I'll try not to get in your way. Where do you want the box?"

"What? Oh, the bedroom, I guess," he answered distractedly. He'd been paying more attention to her slender legs, revealed so invitingly in a pair of crisp white shorts, than he had to what she was saying. "And please, feel free to come and go any time. You won't bother me." Not in the way she meant, anyway.

She paused on the second-floor landing. "The master bedroom?"

"Actually I think I'll take the one right here at the top of the stairs," he said, making a split-second decision. "It was my room when I was a kid." And he preferred it to the larger bedroom, which he still thought of as Chester's.

"Oh." Stacey blushed prettily as, with seeming reluctance, she entered the door he pointed to.

Alex immediately saw why she was uncomfortable. She'd been sleeping in this room. Her fresh, airy scent was all over it. The dresser was littered with feminine paraphernalia—perfume bottles, nail polish, hair ribbons. And the bed—the sheets were still rumpled from the impression her body had made sleeping among them.

She set the box down on the floor and hastily smoothed the covers up over the pillows. "I guess you can see—well, I just haven't had time to move everything out yet. I've emptied the closet and the dresser, but—"

"Don't worry about it. There's no hurry." This time, when he felt the impulse to touch her, to soothe her anxiety, he gave in to it. But the moment his hand came into contact with the smooth skin of her upper arm, he knew he'd made a mistake. The tactile sensations, her scent, the questioning look in her sky-blue eyes, and the proximity of a soft bed conspired against him. The sudden rush of tightness in his lower body took him completely by surprise.

Cautiously he pulled his hand away and cleared his throat. "I'll go get those other boxes."

As soon as he was gone, Stacey quickly stripped the bed and tried not to think about the way Alex had just looked at her—like he was a hungry cat and she a plump mouse—or the oddly delicious, warm glow that look had given her.

She bundled up the sheets and blankets and had started out the door, toward the bathroom where the laundry chute was located, when she heard her daughter's plaintive call. She dropped the sheets in the doorway and strode quickly to the little dormer room, with its pretty maple furniture and rosebud wallpaper. "Can't breathe," Emily announced from the bed, where she'd made a nest for herself among the white eyelet sheets and a herd of stuffed toys.

Stacey plucked a tissue from the box on the nightstand and held it to Emily's nose. "Blow." She did. "Feeling any better?"

Emily shrugged. The fact that she hadn't balked at staying in bed was evidence enough that the cold she'd caught was getting her down. Stacey felt the little girl's forehead; she didn't seem unduly warm. "Do your ears hurt?" she asked.

Emily shook her head as she took a sip from a cup of orange juice.

"What about your throat?"

"No." Emily set the cup back on her nightstand. "Read me?"

Whenever Emily resorted to baby talk, Stacey knew the child needed some mothering. She glanced at her watch and quickly decided everything else could wait. "A short one," she agreed.

As if by magic, Emily produced a dog-eared picture book. Stacey had read it aloud so many times that she had the text memorized, and so did Emily for that matter, but she never tired of it.

Stacey opened to the first page and began: "Once upon a time there was a dog named Sam..." She stopped when she sensed, rather than saw, another presence in the room. When she looked up, Alex was standing in the doorway.

At her wordless invitation, he stepped in, looking larger than life against the bedroom's diminutive proportions. "What have we here?" he asked, his attention focused on Emily.

"I'm sick," Emily announced, as if it were a great privilege. "Mommy's reading me a story."

"I can see that." He gave Stacey a questioning look.

"It's just a case of the sniffles," she said in answer to his unasked question, "but the doctor said to keep her in bed."

Alex looked undeniably relieved. "Oh, Stacey, someone's on the phone for you downstairs. A, um, Prince Charming?"

She laughed. "That's 'Prints Charming,' P-R-I-N-T-S," she clarified. "The printer who does my newsletter. I better go see what they want."

"But Mommy, you're *reading!*" Emily objected.

"I'll be back in a minute," Stacey said, absently handing the book to Alex as she stood.

Emily didn't look pleased. "Then you read," she said, pointing to Alex.

Alex looked momentarily nonplussed, but then a slow smile spread across his face. "Sure, I can take over," he offered, shooing Stacey toward the door.

"Oh—if you don't mind... are you sure?"

"This is one of my favorite authors," he assured her as he lowered himself into the rocking chair.

With a grateful smile Stacey left the room and hurried downstairs followed by the sound of Alex's deep voice describing the adventures of Sam the Dog.

She was a bit out of breath by the time she reached the phone in the kitchen. "Stacey Kidd. Sorry to keep you waiting."

"That's okay." It was Larry, the pressman.

"Is there a problem?" *Oh, please, don't let there be a problem,* she prayed. Her move to Topeka had put enough kinks in her production schedule. She hadn't allowed any extra time for goof-ups.

"No, no," he quickly assured her. "I just wanted to let you know that the newsletter is done and on its way to the mailing house. Since we're a couple of days early, I wanted to make sure you'd sent the mailing labels already."

"I sent them yesterday," she replied, breathing a sigh of relief. The seven thousand labels were the last thing she'd printed out on her computer before she'd dismantled the system and toted it upstairs to the attic apartment.

"Great. Sorry to bother you, then."

"Oh, I don't mind being bothered, as long as it's good news." She'd been extremely impressed with her new Topeka printer, but she had reservations about the mailing house she'd contracted. They'd seemed eager to please and had given her an excellent bid, but once she'd agreed to use them, their service level had dropped considerably.

By the time she returned upstairs, the story was winding down and so was Emily. Her eyelids drooped even as she tried to fight sleep. "'Nother one," she said.

"How about later?" Stacey leaned over her daughter to plant a quick kiss on her forehead. And to Alex, Stacey said, "She didn't get much sleep last night."

"And that means you didn't, either," he said as he stood.

She shrugged. "I'm used to it."

"You can go now," Emily said graciously as she snuggled under her quilt. "I'll talk to Chester if I get lonely."

Alex's eyebrows flew up at that, but he didn't speak until they were out the door and down the hall. "Chester?"

"No need for you to go into shock. I showed her your grandfather's picture and explained that he'd given us the house. But she's too young to understand the concept of death, so she invented an imaginary playmate and called him Chester. She has a very vivid imagination."

Alex seemed to accept the explanation. "Is she always so bossy?" he asked with a teasing grin.

Stacey nodded. "She can be as obstinate as a bull when she wants to be. Thanks for reading to her. She didn't ask very politely."

"Really, she's a good kid," he concluded. He wore an odd, wistful expression that made Stacey wonder if he wasn't thinking of the children he and Jeanne might have had, if given the chance. How lonely her life would be without Emily, she thought with a pang of compassion.

"Well, I guess we better keep working." She headed briskly toward the front door.

"It's all done," Alex said. "All but your things."

She stopped and groaned at the reminder. She'd moved as much as she could by herself, but there was still the furniture. "Are you sure you don't mind helping me?"

"How would it get done if I didn't?" he countered.

"Good point. Will you let me buy pizza for lunch?"

"That's a deal. I assume that huge pile of stuff in the salon is yours?"

She nodded. "The salon, huh? I was wondering what to call that room." She led the way through the French doors off the living room and into the room in question. She'd instructed the movers to put all of her possessions in one area, so that it would be easier to keep her things separate from Alex's when he moved out. If she'd known then how the living arrangements were going to work out, she'd have had everything moved to the attic in the first place.

"This doesn't look too bad," Alex said, surveying the stack of furnishings that included two beds, a small sofa, a table and chairs, two file cabinets—and a desk. A huge desk. "Does that thing come apart?"

Stacey shook her head. "'Fraid not. It's solid as the oak tree it came from."

"Hmm. Well, let's save it till last. The rest we can manage, if you're as strong as you say you are."

She flexed her muscles for him. "That's brute strength you're looking at."

It was the shapeliest, smoothest brute strength he'd ever seen, he thought with a grin, though he stopped just sort of expressing that opinion aloud. "Come on, then, let's see what you're made of."

As they wrestled mattresses and box springs up two flights of stairs, Alex had to admit that she was one tough lady. Headboards and bed rails followed. She never shrank from a heavy load—she even managed one end of the sofa—and it seemed she never would tire, either. In fact, he was the one who had to rest on the second-floor landing, huffing and puffing, while she appeared only slightly flushed.

"Don't tell me," he said between gasps for air. "You do aerobics, right?"

"With a video," she replied. "Emily and I work out together, but I guess we'll have to forego our exercise routine for a while. I didn't bring the VCR with me—it's Mom's."

"You can use mine," he offered automatically, then wished he hadn't. If he ever caught sight of Stacey in one of those French-cut leotards... Damn, his imagination was working overtime where she was concerned. He shook his head to clear it. "Ready to tackle the attic stairs?" he asked.

She gave him a crisp salute and a disarming smile. "Aye, aye." On the count of three they hoisted the sofa and, with several complicated maneuvers, managed to get it up the final flight of steps.

The two-bedroom apartment was filling up fast, Alex noticed. He wondered how she'd manage, with herself, Emily, and a business all tucked under the eaves. He wasn't even sure what her business entailed. She'd said something about a newsletter, and she had a fairly sophisticated computer system. He would ask her about it later. Maybe the publication was something his clients would want to advertise in.

Finally only the desk remained downstairs. Even with its drawers and glass top removed, it was still heavy as a hunk of granite.

They pushed and pulled, heaved and cursed and finally bullied the thing up to the second floor. As they rested, Alex studied the narrow attic stairs, then the desk, and shook his head.

"It'll never make that turn," he said.

"But it has to," Stacey insisted. "I have to have a desk."

"We can try. Maybe if we turn it on end..."

She rubbed her hands together. "I'm sure we can manage it somehow. Let's go."

Unfortunately even Stacey's enthusiasm couldn't rewrite the laws of geometry. The desk became wedged where the stairs turned, and nothing short of an ax was going to get it around the corner.

Defeated, Stacey sank onto the stairs, running her hand over the glossy oak finish on one of the desk's well-turned legs. "Well, I guess that's that. I'll have to store it in the basement. I can work on the dining room table for a while, I suppose."

The thought of lugging the beast down two-and-a-half flights of stairs made Alex blanche. He searched for another solution to Stacey's predicament and arrived at one almost immediately. "I have an idea. Why don't you turn one of the second-floor bedrooms into an office?"

Stacey brightened for a moment, but then her face fell. "I couldn't impose."

"Why not? The bedroom at the end of the hall is empty, and I sure won't need it."

"But I'd hate to be underfoot—"

"I'm gone most of the time," he said. "You couldn't possibly get in the way."

"We'd have to make some adjustment to the rent, wouldn't you say?"

He waved away her concern. "We can work that out later."

Before she could make any further objections, she found herself gripping her end of the desk and coaxing it back down to the second floor. They barely managed to squeeze it through the bedroom doorway, and then Stacey ended up trapped behind the massive piece of furniture as they slid it into place against one wall.

There was no way to crawl under it; her only means of escape was over the top. "Help me out, would you please?" she asked, exasperated by the fact that Alex had made no move to assist her. He just stood and grinned at her, apparently enjoying her dilemma.

Finally he offered her a hand for support. She took it, blatantly enjoying the strength and warmth of his touch as he helped her clamor over the top of the desk. His hands went to her waist to assist her to the floor. When she was safely on her feet again, however, he didn't release her.

She looked up, questioning, but once she saw the hungry look in his hazel eyes she had no need to ask. Involuntarily she took a quick, deep breath, feeling his hands tighten around her waist.

It didn't occur to her to try to escape. She sensed it wouldn't have done any good, anyway; her fate was sealed. She knew just how a mouse feels when the cat stops toying with its prey and closes in for the kill.

Still, he didn't claim his prize right away. His eyes took inventory of her face, cataloguing its assets, perhaps, or calculating from which front he would make his final assault.

Stacey grew impatient for the inevitable as the seconds stretched between them. She grasped his strong shoulders, raised up on her toes and planted her lips firmly against his.

Alex groaned his approval. He slid one hand down to her hip and pulled her closer, fitting her softness against his hardness. With his other hand he lightly grazed her back on an upward path, raising goose bumps on every square inch of her flesh. His body radiated a pleasant warmth from their recent exertions.

The kiss was urgent yet thorough, intense in its impact but almost leisurely in pace. His tongue sought entrance to her mouth and she readily obliged him, delighting in the curious exploration. All the while his hands never ceased their movements, stroking her back, massaging, tangling in her thick hair.

She'd never before lost herself so completely in a man's arms. At the same time, she'd never felt so completely at home. This seemed right, so right—

"Mommy? *Mother!*"

At the sound of Emily's impatient summons from across the hall, Alex and Stacey sprang apart. The effect was not unlike a dousing with a bucket of cold water.

Stacey looked everywhere but at him. "I'd better go see what she wants," she muttered, grateful for an excuse to flee the room. As she hurried down the hall toward Emily, her heart still pounding erratically, she mentally kicked herself all the way to China.

What had gotten into her? Had she been without male companionship for so long that she would melt into the embrace of any man who came along? She hadn't even dated since Rich had left her—hadn't wanted or needed to. Between Emily and her mother and her newsletter, her life was full. But maybe she'd denied herself for too long. Her mother certainly hinted often enough that Stacey ought to have a man in her life. If she was so physically and emotionally needy that she behaved like... like...

But Alex wasn't just "any man," she conceded. There was something profound in the way his kiss had made her feel, something that went far beyond mere physical need. Not just any man would make her feel so strange, so wonderful—or so scared.

"Mommy, your face is red," Emily said when Stacey entered the small bedroom.

"I don't doubt it," Stacey replied, then added, "it's a warm day today. Watcha need?" She felt her daughter's forehead. It was still reassuringly cool.

"I'm hungry."

Stacey glanced at her watch, shocked to see that it was almost one o'clock. "Well, no wonder! It's way past lunchtime. How do you feel about pizza?"

Emily nodded enthusiastically.

Just then Alex stuck his head inside the door. "Did someone say pizza? What kind should we get?" He looked as normal as could be—as if the kiss had never happened—which was annoying, since Stacey still felt flushed and tongue-tied.

"Hamburger," Emily stated emphatically. "I don't like any other kind."

"But maybe Alex doesn't like hamburger, sweetheart," Stacey said diplomatically.

"It's my favorite," he assured them. "I'll go downstairs and call it in."

Stacey put the portable TV on the foot of Emily's bed and managed to get her interested in cartoons. Then she took the empty orange juice cup, intending to go down to the kitchen and refill it. But as she passed the open door to Alex's room she spied the forgotten pile of sheets.

Darn it, she had to get her things out of there so he could settle in. She stepped inside and gathered up the sheets. As she started to leave, something caught her eye. One of Alex's boxes sat on the bare mattress, open to reveal the contents. Sitting right on top was a small, mother-of-pearl picture frame. Inside the frame was a photo of a woman—a beautiful woman, with an impish smile, large, dark eyes, and a mass of black curls tumbling all around her face.

Jeanne, Alex's wife.

She felt an odd pressure behind her eyes and realized she wanted to cry for the death of this woman she'd never known. He must have loved Jeanne a lot; he obviously still felt the loss keenly.

Stacey wasn't a stranger to loss. Rich had abandoned her, after all, and that had been a hard, bitter pill to swallow. But deep down, even through the haze of pain, she'd known it was for the best. They hadn't been in love for a long time. She couldn't imagine what it would be like to have someone you were in love with suddenly stripped from you.

Of course, she had no idea whether the woman's death had been sudden. Regardless, she'd have to watch her step from now on. She had no intention of auditioning for the part of Jeanne's replacement.

Downstairs, Alex hung up the phone, leaned against the kitchen counter and sighed deeply. He'd sought to occupy his mind and body with anything—anything—to distract him from memories of kissing Stacey Kidd. But a simple phone call to the local pizza emporium hadn't done the trick.

He hadn't intended to hold onto her like that. But she'd been so suddenly close, and her proximity had been hard—no, impossible—to resist. As he'd held her, suspended in time for uncounted moments, he'd studied her face, trying to find some trace of displeasure. If he'd sensed rejection from her, he could have let her go. But all he'd seen was an expression of surprise and wonder.

He'd actually tried to think of Jeanne, but his mind had been too full of Stacey—flesh and blood, present-tense Stacey. When she'd impatiently closed the distance between them, he'd thought of nothing except how good she felt against him, warm and alive and full of feminine mystery.

Thank heavens the little munchkin had interrupted them when she had. Now that he'd been singed by the fire between himself and Stacey, he'd be more wary. In another time, another place, he might have pursued her with everything he had. But he wasn't ready.

It wasn't that he still mourned. He'd accepted Jeanne's absence from his life, although he still missed her sometimes. Neither did he feel disloyal, not exactly. Jeanne would have been the first to encourage him to live again, to love again, and five years was a long time.

But something still held him back—a sense that some part of his past relationship with his wife had been left unfinished. Until he figured out what it was and put it to rest, he couldn't consider anything more than friendship with his sexy landlady.

The doorbell rang. He glanced at his watch. It couldn't be the pizza already.

"I'll get it," Stacey's melodious voice sang out. He heard her bare feet thumping across the wood floor toward the front door.

Curious, he went to see who was paying them a call. He hung back, observing Stacey as she talked with the uniformed delivery man.

"I think there's been a mistake," she said, obviously agitated. "Those were supposed to go to Stubbs Mailing House."

"Yes, ma'am, but there's a problem," the visitor explained patiently. "Seems that the mailing house has quit business. The doors are locked and there's an official notice on their front door. They've gone bankrupt."

"Is there something I can do?" Alex asked as he stepped forward.

Stacey turned to him, looking defeated. "Just stay in a tolerant frame of mind," she said, her voice full of despair. "We've got to find a place to stack seven thousand newsletters. And somehow I have to get them labeled and delivered to the post office before Monday."

Alex groaned inwardly. *You couldn't possibly get in my way.* He'd uttered those words less than an hour ago, and already he could see himself tripping over the boxes.

Still, he knew he'd pitch in and help her. She looked so distraught, he'd have done just about anything to make her smile again. "For now we can put them in the salon, where your furniture was," he said.

She shot him a grateful smile before instructing the delivery man where to stack the boxes.

There was only one consolation, Alex mused. If they had to spend the rest of the weekend sticking address labels on newsletters, they'd be too busy to engage in any more stolen kisses.

Chapter Four

"What is this thing you publish, anyway?" Alex asked as he used his pocket knife to open one of the boxes at random.

"It's a newsletter for new parents," Stacey answered with a note of pride. Her latest issue of *Baby Chatter* was a high-quality publication, a far cry from her first, single-page photocopied effort of more than two years ago. She couldn't help but be proud of how far she'd come.

Alex silently studied the pink-and-blue cover, then nodded appreciatively. "Pretty slick. Does it read as good as it looks?"

"Of course." Then she wilted. "But no one's going to read it if I don't figure out how to get it labeled and to the post office."

"I'm sure another mailing house would jump at the chance—"

But Stacey just shook her head. "It was hard enough finding a bindery and mailing house that would take this job under any circumstances. No one will accept it on short notice."

"It's only seven thousand pieces," Alex reasoned.

"Seven thousand custom-bound pieces," Stacey elaborated. "All of the newsletters have the same front and back pages. But the middle pages are customized for the age of the baby. There's a newborn insert, a one-month insert—all the way until the baby is a year old."

"So you have twelve newsletters each month instead of one?" Alex asked, nodding his understanding. "What a clever marketing strategy. Where do you get your mailing list?"

"I've hooked up with hospital maternity programs all over the country," she explained. "They offer *Baby Chatter* as one of their benefits, right along with free diapers and discounts on baby clothes."

"And it's working? I mean, it's a successful venture?"

"Until this moment, yes!" she said, hearing the edge of desperation in her own voice. "But I'm under contract to get them in the mail by Monday, and—"

"Don't worry, we'll take care of it," he said soothingly. "I can call some people who work for me. We'll get an assembly line going—no problem."

Stacey made a concerted effort to quell her panic. Alex offered a potential solution to her problem, if she could just iron out the details. "Do you think you can find about eight pairs of hands?" she asked. "Counting you and me, that would be seven hundred pieces each, stuffed, folded, labeled, and sorted. We could do it in two afternoons."

Again, he appeared impressed. "You have the process down, don't you."

"I used to do it all myself, before the list got too big to manage on my own. I know how long it takes, down to the minute. I'll pay your people, of course... um, how much will they want per hour?" She hoped her anxiety didn't show through, but discussions of money always unnerved her—particularly when she was in a spot like this, where she had no choice and little in the way of reserve funds.

"It'll cost you no more than you would have paid the mailing house," he replied.

"How can you be sure?"

"Because I'm giving you my word." He went to the kitchen to make some phone calls without waiting for her to agree to his plan.

He was patronizing her and she knew it. Already she owed him some sort of rent refund for the use of his extra bedroom as an office, yet he had avoided discussing the exact amount. *Don't worry about it,* he'd said. Now he was blithely informing her that he would solve this dilemma, too.

Darn it, she hated being rescued, like some wimpy damsel in distress. Building this business with her own two hands had gone a long way toward restoring the self-confidence that Rich had torn down. She didn't need a macho man taking over for her, patting her head and telling her everything would work out fine.

Whoa, girl, she cautioned herself. Alex was just trying to help her out of a jam. She'd be crazy to turn down assistance she desperately needed. She would simply make sure that she paid him and his workers a reasonable amount for the job, and that would be that.

Twenty minutes later Alex had committed six people willing to help. The pizza arrived just as Stacey got off the phone from tracking down the mailing labels she'd sent to Stubbs yesterday. She grabbed her purse and ran to the door, but Alex beat her to it. He had already paid the delivery boy by the time she'd pulled the money out of her purse.

"This was supposed to be my treat, remember?" she said.

He waved away her concern. "Mmm, this smells great. Shall we take it up to Emily's room?"

She bit her tongue to keep from arguing. The man was impossible. "All right. I'll get some plates and things."

When she headed up the stairs a couple of minutes later, she found Alex standing in the hallway, his finger to his lips. "Shh. She's conked out."

Stacey sighed. "I suppose it's best to let her sleep," she whispered back. "She'll be hungry and grumbly when she wakes up, though."

"Has she seen a doctor?" Alex asked as they went back downstairs.

"No, but I called her pediatrician in Kansas City. Rest, fluids, kiddie decongestant, and TLC—that's about all you can do for a cold."

"Does she catch cold often?" Alex asked as he set the pizza on the dining room table and opened the box.

"Less often than most kids, actually. Since she's not in day care, she's not exposed to as many germs. You want parmesan on yours?" Stacey asked as she opened the small plastic container of cheese that had come with the pizza.

Alex nodded. They lapsed into silence, communicating only through nods of satisfaction as they worked their way through gooey cheese and tangy tomato sauce. Stacey hadn't realized how hungry she was until she'd demolished three pieces. Finally she threw down her napkin and issued a contented sigh.

"You have tomato sauce on your cheek," Alex said just before popping his last bite of crust into his mouth.

"Where?" She rubbed her face. "I've shared too many meals with just Emily," she said with a laugh. "I think I've forgotten the social niceties, like not wearing my food. I didn't talk with my mouth full, did I?"

Obviously she'd missed the spot, because Alex smiled indulgently and dabbed at her cheek with a clean napkin. The gesture should have made her feel all of three years old, but instead his touch gave her a sudden awareness of how close they sat and how very much a woman she was.

Her skin tingled where his fingertips had brushed against her face, though he'd long since pulled his hand away. Now his hazel eyes locked onto hers, and the image of their unexpected kiss came crashing into the forefront of her memory. Acutely aware of the masculine aura of warmth that surrounded Alex, she remembered how it had felt to let that aura envelop her, to let his arms surround her, to feel the urgency of his mouth against hers.

Looking into his eyes, she was sure that he recalled the kiss as clearly as she did, and that he felt just as uncertain about it.

The doorbell rang. Stacey shook her head to break the spell and even dared to smile when she saw Alex doing the same thing. "I'll get it," she said as she hopped up quickly from her chair.

A woman from a delivery service had brought Stacey her mailing labels. Standing behind her on the front porch were the first of the "rescue squad" Alex had pulled together, his partner's two teenaged daughters.

"Am I glad to see you—all of you," Stacey greeted them as she signed for the delivery.

It took her only a few minutes to organize the assembly line. By then the other four workers had arrived: two secretaries from Alex's office, and two of his advertising salespersons—a bespectacled young man with a bow tie and a very beautiful, very pregnant woman.

Hasty introductions were made, but little time was wasted on social niceties. Everyone seemed eager to work, much to Stacey's relief. She quickly outlined her needs, and the stuffing, stapling, labeling, and sorting began. By late afternoon, when two more pizzas mysteriously arrived, she estimated that they'd taken care of almost two thousand.

"You people are terrific," she congratulated them as they took a break from the tedious work to enjoy their pizza. Since she'd already eaten, she took the opportunity to check on Emily, who had been ominously quiet. Earlier she had awakened, briefly, to eat a few bites, but then had fallen right back to sleep.

She woke up as soon as Stacey entered the small bedroom. "Mommy, I don't feel good," she whimpered.

Stacey felt the child's forehead, then took her temperature to be sure, but she didn't have a fever. "You'll get better soon," Stacey soothed as she dosed her daughter with a children's cold medicine.

"Is she worse?" Alex asked from the doorway.

Stacey had to smile at the furrow of concern between his eyebrows. He obviously wasn't used to children, or he wouldn't be so worried over a case of the sniffles. "She's fine, just a stuffy nose."

"No, Mommy, I'm terrible sick," Emily objected.

Stacey assumed a serious expression. "Well, if you're that sick, maybe we better go to the doctor."

Emily's china blue eyes grew large as she pulled the covers protectively over herself. "No! I'm not *that* sick, and I don't need a shot."

Stacey smiled and ruffled her daughter's wispy blond hair. "Good. Would you like to come downstairs for a while and watch us work?"

Emily nodded.

"Are you sure she should be out of bed?" Alex asked as Stacey wrestled with Emily's slippers.

"Good heavens, Alex, the kid's been in bed all day. She'll perish from boredom if I don't let her up for a little while." She wrapped Emily up in a quilt and grabbed her favorite purple teddy bear before carrying her downstairs.

The others made the expected fuss over Emily as Stacey settled her into an overstuffed chair, tucking the quilt around her, but they quickly returned to their respective tasks.

Alex was now working right next to her after switching jobs with one of the teenagers, Stacey noted, not quite sure how she felt about his nearness. She'd managed to recover all right from their last encounter, but he was close enough that she could detect the scent of his aftershave, and that unnerved her.

"So how did you get started with *Baby Chatter?*" he asked.

She was relieved that at least he'd chosen a comfortable topic of conversation. "I sort of fell into it by accident. I had almost earned a journalism degree at University of Kansas when I had to drop out. So I—"

"Why'd you drop out?" he asked.

She nodded covertly toward Emily.

"Oh, I see."

"I went into labor during finals, for what would have been my second-to-last semester," she elaborated. "The pains were coming four minutes apart, but I refused to get up out of that chair until I'd finished my Communications Law exam. I was scared to death I'd have to take that class over." She shrugged and felt her face flushing. She was amazed she'd told Alex something so personal. At least no one else in the room appeared to be listening in. They were all involved in their own conversations.

"I think you would have been excused, under the circumstances," he said.

"Probably," she mumbled. "It didn't matter anyway, since I never went back to school."

"Why didn't you?"

"I thought it was important to stay home with my baby," she answered. "I still do. I just couldn't face turning Emily over to strangers to raise. Oh, I know that in this day and age, most mothers have to work, and I certainly don't blame them for turning to day care or baby-sitters, but I was lucky enough to have an alternative."

"Meaning your husband earned enough money that you could afford to stay home?"

She gave a derisive laugh at that. "No, not my husband. He'd already divorced me by the time Emily was born. My mother is the one who opened her home to us."

But Alex was still recovering from her announcement about her husband. "What kind of a jerk would divorce a pregnant wife?" he asked with obvious, utter disgust. But then he realized what he'd asked and backpedaled. "I'm sorry, that's none of my business."

Stacey answered him, anyway. "He was a very unhappy man, and I just didn't provide whatever it was he needed in a wife, I guess. We didn't plan for a baby so soon, but when it happened I thought it would pull us together. I tried to reconcile him to the idea of having a family, but..." She shook her head. "Poor Rich."

"Poor Rich? What about poor Stacey?"

"I'm the lucky one. I have Emily."

A smile softened Alex's face. "Yeah, I guess you're right. So, the newsletter?" he asked, prompting her to continue.

"Oh, right. My mother is an administrator at Woodland Memorial Hospital, and when the PR department needed a freelance writer, she suggested me. Then the hospital asked me to write a leaflet for their maternity patients, and somehow that expanded into a monthly newsletter."

"Obviously you were smart enough to retain the rights to it."

She nodded. "Pretty soon I was contracting with hospitals all over the area, and then whole chains of hospitals around the country—it just mushroomed. And I can do almost all the work from home."

"Who sells your advertising?"

"I do. I do everything—I assign the stories, edit them, set the type, lay out the pages."

"Hmm."

"Hmm what?"

"Have you ever thought of hiring an account executive to sell your ads?" he asked, thumbing through the pages of the newsletter he was supposed to be stapling together. "You've got some good solid accounts here, but you could do better. A lot of advertisers would pay dearly for your mailing list—it's extremely specific and updated monthly."

"And you think a trained salesperson could sell more ads?" Stacey asked. "I'll admit, sales isn't one of my strongest suits."

"Hmm," Alex said again.

"What? Would you stop saying 'Hmm' and tell me what you're thinking?"

He nodded toward the pregnant woman. "Ramona is leaving my agency as soon as she delivers," he said. "Like you, she thinks it's important to stay home with her baby. But she was saying just the other day that she'd like to find some kind of work that she could do from home."

"She could sell ads over the phone," Stacey agreed excitedly. "Oh, but I'm getting ahead of myself," she added in a more sober tone.

"What's wrong?"

"I can't exactly afford an employee. I'm finally making a profit, but—"

"That's the beauty of a salesperson," Alex interrupted her. "She'll work on straight commission. That way she can't possibly cost more than she makes for you."

Stacey brightened. "When you put it that way...I'll talk to Ramona. Are you sure it's okay? I feel like I'm stealing one of your employees."

He nodded. "I'm sure."

Stacey returned to her task of sticking on labels with renewed vigor. She suddenly felt much better about everything. If she could reassemble this team tomorrow, the newsletters would be to the post office in plenty of time. Emily was obviously feeling better, happily ensconced in her easy chair and reading a picture book to her teddy bear. And Alex—well, she found Alex surprisingly easy to talk to. She'd told him things she seldom mentioned to anyone, even her mother, and she didn't feel at all embarrassed about it.

As for that kiss, it didn't mean anything. Alex was just a man, a very nice man. The embrace had been a fluke, a nervous reaction caused by an accidental collision of bodies. Now that they were getting to know one another, she was sure it wouldn't be repeated.

She offered him a tremulous smile, which he returned in kind. "So, how did you get into the advertising business?" she asked, suddenly wanting to learn as much about him as she'd just revealed about herself.

"By accident, same as you," he said. "There was a pretty girl at registration, waiting in line to sign up for Marketing 101. I stepped out of the Introduction to Geology line so I could stand behind her. Then I found out I liked marketing, so I switched majors."

"And all those rocks had to get along without you," Stacey teased. "What about the girl?"

The smile dropped abruptly from Alex's face. "I married her."

"Oh." Where did she go from here? Stacey wondered. To continue the conversation in the same vein might be uncomfortable, but dropping the subject like a hot potato was even more awkward. "So, you got a marketing degree," she continued carefully. "Did you go to work for an advertising agency right away?"

"No, Jeanne and I formed our own agency," he said gruffly.

Damn, she'd done it again. "Would you like me to shut up?"

"If you don't mind— I mean, I really can't talk about her, not today."

"No problem," Stacey said, feeling as if she'd just had a door slammed in her face. The closeness she'd started to feel with Alex evaporated like morning dew. She had opened up to him, trusted him, yet he apparently didn't trust her to the same degree.

Her annoyance didn't last long. Alex was hurting, after all. His defensiveness wasn't a calculated response; it was just something that happened. She'd behaved much the same way when people prodded her to talk about her marriage or her divorce, when the hurt was still fresh.

But Jeanne had been gone five years. What in the world could cause him to carry his pain for so long?

The doorbell rang, putting an end to her speculation. She laid down her stack of labels and started for the door, but again Alex got there first. She waited to see who the caller was.

A good-looking young man with sandy hair and wire glasses entered the foyer—someone who was apparently well-known to Alex as the two men shook hands warmly. Satisfied, she started to turn back toward her labels.

"Stacey," Alex called. "There's someone here I'd like you to meet."

She rose to answer his summons, only mildly irritated at the pile of newsletters stacking up, waiting to be stapled. He was going to foul up the whole system if he wasn't careful.

She smiled and extended her hand to the man, who did likewise when Alex introduced him as Paul Gibbs.

But the smile froze on her face when she saw the black leather bag he held in his other hand.

"Paul is a pediatrician," Alex said, confirming her suspicions. "He's also an old friend of mine. I thought you might want him to take a look at Emily."

She stiffened in outrage. How dare he? How dare Alex send for a doctor without clearing it with her? But the last thing she needed to do was lose her temper when she had a house full of guests. And the poor hapless doctor—this wasn't his fault. She shouldn't take out her wrath on him.

"How kind of you to come," she said to Paul through gritted teeth, then couldn't help adding, "though it really wasn't necessary. She just has a cold. Still, as long as you're here..." She led the way into the living room, where Emily eyed the newcomer with overt suspicion. Stacey's normally friendly, cheerful daughter turned into a pint-sized ogre whenever a doctor came within a hundred feet of her.

Paul hunkered down until he was at Emily's level. "Hi, I'm Dr. Gibbs, and you must be Emily."

Emily folded her arms and stared accusingly at her mother. "What's he doing here?"

Paul's eyebrows shot up, and he hid an amused smile behind his hand for a moment before he regained his composure. "So, you don't like doctors?" he asked the child.

"No," Emily answered unequivocally.

"Emily..." Stacey warned, but Paul shook his head, as if to say he could handle it.

"I know sometimes doctors aren't much fun, but they can also make you feel better when you're sick," he said.

Emily frowned as she considered this. "Do you have a shot in there?" she asked, pointing to the black bag.

Paul made a show of searching the bag. "No, but—I'll be darned. There's a monkey in here."

"Really? Let me see."

Surprised and pleased that the doctor was winning over her daughter, Stacey returned her attention to Alex, staring at him through slitted eyes. She longed to give him the tongue-lashing he deserved, but she'd have to wait until they were alone.

After another minute or two, Emily agreed to let the doctor examine her. Stacey picked up the girl and carried her into the kitchen, where the light was better and they would have some privacy, pointedly closing the door in Alex's face when he tried to follow.

The exam was brief but thorough, and Emily was surprisingly compliant, though her lips were pressed together grimly. When he was done, Paul turned to Stacey and said, with mock gravity, "Well, Stacey, your daughter has a head cold."

Stacey couldn't help but laugh. "No kidding."

"Seriously, she looks good—no lung congestion, ears look fine, throat looks fine, no fever. I assume you're giving her an over-the-counter children's remedy of some sort?"

Stacey nodded.

"I don't think there's any need to prescribe medication. Just make sure she gets plenty of rest—" He stopped when Emily pulled on his sleeve.

"You forgot," she said gravely.

"Forgot? Oh, your monkey, right." He opened his bag again and rummaged around inside. "Green or red?"

"Green," she said decisively.

Stacey expected him to produce the standard doctor's bribe of a lollipop. Instead he extracted a long balloon from his bag and proceeded to blow it up. With deft hands he contorted the balloon into the shape of a monkey. "Be careful with it," he cautioned Emily as he handed it to her. "If it pops, throw it in the trash. Promise?"

She nodded, obviously delighted with her present. She even remembered to thank the doctor. Then she asked Stacey, "Can I show Uncle Alex?"

Uncle Alex? "Sure," Stacey replied as she set Emily on the floor. The child made a hasty exit.

"Feel free to call me if she gets worse," Paul said, handing Stacey his card.

"Thank you. You really are good with her, and I'll be needing a pediatrician here in Topeka, so I'm sure I'll call you. Um, how much do I owe you for this little extravagance?"

Paul quickly shook his head. "It's on the house. I owe Alex a favor or two. In fact, I think I owe him another for introducing me to such a pretty lady."

Stacey stared at her toes and blushed furiously. This was all she needed right now. "Er, I'll walk you to the door," she mumbled as she headed into the living room, her head still bent low. As she passed Alex, who sat in the easy chair with Emily in his lap, she glared meaningfully at him. He responded with raised eyebrows and an expression of complete innocence.

"Don't get up, Alex," Paul said over his shoulder as he headed for the door. "I'll see you later." And to Stacey he said in a lower voice, "Don't be too hard on him."

"What to you mean?" she asked stiffly.

"You don't hide your feelings very well. You obviously weren't very pleased to see me, and if looks could kill, Alex would be a candidate for the undertaker."

There was no use denying what the good doctor had observed, so she didn't try. Instead she stepped outside onto the porch with Paul, then gave him her hand. "I'm sorry you came out here for nothing."

"It wasn't for nothing. Alex was worried."

"It's not his place," she said hotly, unable to hold back the anger any longer. "Emily's mine. If anyone's going to worry, I'll worry."

"And I'm sure you'll do a damn fine job of it, too," Paul said with a teasing smile. But then he sobered. "Alex meant well. Remember that."

Stacey tried to heed Paul's warning, but it was no use. She was still furious by the time the workers cleared out, with promises to return tomorrow and finish the job.

"We got quite a lot done," Alex declared when they were alone.

"Yes," she agreed tersely. "Thank you. I'm tired now. I'm going to bed." Before she could say something she couldn't take back, she left the room—so quickly Alex could do nothing more than stare after her in surprise.

She tried to work off her anger by energetically setting up Emily's bed in the third-floor apartment, but even after she had bid her protesting daughter goodnight, she still wanted to kick something.

Maybe by tomorrow she would be able to put things into perspective, she thought as she prepared herself for bed. But Alex didn't give her the chance to cool off. He came knocking at her door.

"Just thought I'd see if you were settled in okay," he said when she opened the door. "Did you get the beds put together?" He tried to peek past her but found his gaze riveted on her slender body encased in a long, shimmery nightgown. Backlit as she was, her gentle curves were plainly revealed to his eyes, and his mouth went suddenly dry.

"Everything is fine," she replied. Her voice sounded as if it were encased in a block of ice. "Good night."

His hand shot out to prevent her from slamming the door in his face—again. "Whoa, wait a minute. Earlier I thought you were ticked off about something, but I was hoping you were just preoccupied. Guess not. Want to talk about it?"

"It's late—"

"Stacey, if we're going to share this house, we have to communicate."

"Oh, you're a fine one to talk about communication."

That threw him for a moment, but then he nodded his understanding. "Is that what you're mad about? That I wouldn't talk about Jeanne?"

She hesitated, then shook her head. "No. If you don't want to talk, that's your right. What *isn't* your right is to call in a doctor for my daughter without bothering to consult me. I told you she didn't need a doctor. Don't you think I'm capable of deciding when my child needs medical attention?"

"I certainly wasn't questioning—"

"I may not be the most savvy businesswoman in the world, and I've made some lousy decisions regarding my personal life, but *no one* can fault me as a mother. Emily comes first in my life—always. I would never put her at risk. Just who do you think you are to second-guess—"

"Stacey, stop it," he said, loudly enough to break through her tirade. "No one said you weren't a good mother. Now for heaven's sake, let me come in and we'll discuss this calmly."

If she'd turned away, he would have let her go this time. But she surprised him by coming out on the landing and closing the door behind her.

"Would you like to yell at me some more," Alex asked as he sat down on the top step, "or would you like to hear my side of the story?"

"I'm sorry, I got carried away," she said, settling on the step next to him, her back straight as a two-by-four.

Good, he thought. At least she appeared to be open to peace talks. "Look, I certainly wasn't questioning your authority or your judgment as a mother. I was just trying to help. I know how hard you're struggling to make ends meet, and I thought that if you did want Emily to see a doctor you might not be able to afford it—" But judging from the outraged expression on Stacey's face, he was just making things worse.

"I am not destitute, I'm just on a tight budget. There is a difference."

"I know, but—"

"Furthermore, I have health insurance. And even if I didn't, I wouldn't allow my financial situation to influence a decision about medical care for my daughter."

Alex stared down the staircase, not really seeing anything. He'd obviously misread the situation. "I'm sorry. I don't know what else to say."

He heard a suspicious sniff from Stacey's direction and turned to find her with her face buried in her hands.

"Stacey?" Reacting on instinct alone, he slid closer to her and put his arm around her shoulders, though earlier he'd vowed to keep his distance from her. "Hey, it's okay. Everything's okay."

"No, it's not," she said, her words muffled against her hands. "I can't believe I just said all those things to you, and after all the help you've given me today— the furniture, the newsletter, Emily..."

"It's okay," he said again. "It's been a long, trying day, and we're adjusting to each other, that's all." He rubbed her shoulders soothingly, letting her long hair tickle the back of his hand. He stopped only when he realized that he'd pressed his face into her hair, and that she was no longer crying.

Abruptly he pulled away. "Feel better?"

She cleared her throat nervously. "Yeah, sure," she said without much conviction.

"Shall we start over again tomorrow, fresh?"

"I think that's a good idea," she said with a nod, and they both stood up. Then she surprised him further by giving him a shaky smile and a brief, hard hug before disappearing inside the apartment.

He could still feel the impression of her warm, supple body against his as he made his way downstairs.

Chapter Five

Stacey sat back on her heels and surveyed the small, cozy living room with satisfaction. Getting her newsletter ready for mailing had taken a big bite out of her schedule, so that she was only now, a week after she'd moved upstairs, able to spend time arranging furniture and hanging pictures. But now that she'd finally settled in, she was quite pleased with the results.

Her things fit like they'd been made for these rooms. The subtle print of her living room furniture upholstery picked up the mint green of the walls; her floral bed linens were made for a pale rose bedroom. Even her dishes went well with the green-and-white kitchen. It was almost as if Chester had known...

No, that was silly.

"Whatcha doin', Mommy?" Emily skipped into the living room, dragging her purple teddy bear by one ear. Her cold had kept her down for a few days, but she was over the worst of it now and had returned to her usual rambunctious self.

"Just admiring," Stacey answered. "What do you think of our new home?"

Emily shrugged. "Can I have a kitten?" she asked as she tried to wiggle her way into her mother's lap.

Inwardly Stacey cringed, even as she pulled her squirming daughter into her arms. She'd thought for sure the kitten had been forgotten. "I don't know. We'll see."

"You always say that," Emily complained.

"We can't get a kitten right now," Stacey reasoned. "When we're all settled in and things get back to normal, we'll look into it." Of course, she wasn't sure anything would ever be normal again. This move had turned her life—not to mention her emotions—topsy-turvy.

"When?" Emily wanted to know.

"May fifteenth," Stacey answered. She had learned that if she gave Emily a definite time to look forward to, she would be satisfied. But like an elephant, she never forgot. Somehow, the kid would know when May fifteenth rolled around, and she would hold Stacey to her promise.

"May fifteenth, May fifteenth," Emily chanted. "Can I have a cookie?"

"Now *that* I can handle," Stacey answered as she pushed herself off the floor. Just this morning she'd been thinking about baking something. "Chocolate chip?"

"Oatmeal," Emily stated definitely. "Please."

"Okay, oatmeal. You want to help me bake them?"

Emily considered this gravely for a moment. "No, I wanta watch cartoons." With that she bounded off.

So much for mother-daughter bonding, Stacey thought with a shake of her head as she made her way to the kitchen.

The tiny, apartment-sized stove was even older than the one downstairs. The burners, she had discovered, had to be lit with a match. Did the oven, too? She wasn't too familiar with gas appliances. She'd always had electric.

She turned the stiff knob on the oven to two-seventy-five and waited hopefully, but nothing happened. There was no hiss or smell of natural gas, and definitely no heat. She turned the knob back to *off* and opened the door, then gasped as something jumped out at her.

It was just a folded piece of paper, she realized with a nervous laugh. But her hand shook as she picked it up. It was another note from Chester:

Dear Stacey,
 At least, I hope it's you reading this. I had this apartment decorated in all your favorite colors, hoping you couldn't resist it.

Now, how did he know her favorite colors, unless her mother was involved? she wondered. But Betty Kidd had steadfastly denied any involvement in Chester's schemes.

 I hope you won't rent the rest of the house to just anyone. Have you thought of Alex? He would make an exemplary tenant, and he would be quite useful to have around—to fix this oven, for example. Think about it.

Yours always,
Chester

Stacey wilted into the nearest chair. This was getting just a little too spooky. How in the world had that old man been able to anticipate her and Alex so accurately? Granted, he probably had known his grandson well enough to guess that if Stacey presented him with the option of moving into the house, he would do it. Alex seemed to be very fond of this white elephant, after all.

"Well, we're way ahead of you, Chester," she murmured, fighting the chill that wiggled down her spine. But his matchmaking scheme still wasn't going to work. A week had gone by since Alex had moved in, and other than that one silly kiss, nothing had happened. More importantly, nothing was *going* to happen. Alex spent a lot of hours at his office, and she was very busy herself. They hardly ever saw each other.

Then why was he constantly in her thoughts?

She absolutely was *not* going to ask him to fix this stupid oven, she vowed. She'd figure it out herself.

Fifteen minutes later she was forced to accept defeat. She knew her computer inside and out, but household appliances weren't her strong suit. She couldn't even find the pilot light, much less figure out how to light it, and the fear that she would blow up the whole house prevented her from experimenting for long.

She was wondering where the Yellow Pages might be, so she could call a repair service, when she heard a ghastly noise just outside the kitchen door, which led out to a small balcony and fire escape. It sounded as if someone was ripping the house apart. She wrenched open the door, then breathed a sigh of relief when she saw it was just Alex. But he did appear to be ripping up the balcony.

"What are you doing out there?" she asked. "You scared me to bits."

"Sorry. The porch and the fire escape have dry rot. They're not safe, so I'm fixing them," he explained.

"Oh. That's...nice of you, Alex. I'd hate to escape a fire, only to break my neck on a rotten stair step."

"Don't joke about things like that," he said, his tone so solemn that she felt immediately guilty. Had Jeanne died in a fire? she wondered, recoiling at the horrible thought. She wasn't about to ask.

"You're right, I shouldn't joke about safety. I should probably review with Emily what to do in a fire, too."

"You mean you haven't?"

"I'll do it today," she said quickly. He was making her feel like a criminal.

"You should have chain ladders for your bedroom windows, too," he said, "in case you can't get to the fire escape. I'll see if I can find some for you."

Again, she wanted to argue that her family's safety wasn't his responsibility, but she bit her tongue. Perhaps he had a reason for being oversensitive about the danger of fire. "Thank you. Now, about these repairs..."

"It won't cost you a thing," he said, reading her mind. "I found a huge pile of new lumber in the basement. I'm sure Chester bought it, intending to fix the stairs, and just never got around to it."

"No, he probably intended for *you* to do it," Stacey said, rolling her eyes heavenward. "He knew you'd be up here on my balcony at the exact moment I needed someone to fix my oven."

Alex laid down his crowbar and leveled his gaze at her. "What are you talking about?"

She sighed. "Oh, it's nothing, really. I found another note from Chester, in the oven of all places. Alex, it's really weird. It's like he knows us so well."

"What did the note say?" he asked as he abandoned his task for the moment. They drifted into the kitchen, and he poured himself a glass of water from the tap.

"He suggested I rent the house to you and live up here."

"You're kidding."

She shook her head.

Alex did the same. "That clever old buzzard. He always managed to get his way, one way or another."

That was hardly a comforting thought, Stacey mused as involuntarily she studied the worn leather tool belt that hung familiarly around Alex's lean hips. She'd caught glimpses of him dressed for work at his office, wearing expensive suits and silk ties, but she preferred him like this, in snug jeans and a faded work shirt, sleeves rolled up to the elbows revealing strong, tanned forearms and capable hands. His hair, which he usually kept neatly combed, was curling a bit in the humidity. There was a tiny cut on his chin, where he'd nicked himself shaving.

"Did you say something about your oven?" he asked.

"Ah, no. I mean, don't worry about it. I'll call someone."

"Doesn't it work? Let me take a look. Maybe it's something simple."

She fought a brief, internal battle, then handed him the flashlight. He was already here, after all, and she could scarcely afford an unnecessary repair bill.

"I think it's just the pilot light. Do you have any matches?" he asked when his head was in the oven. She handed him a matchbook and looked on anxiously, though all she could see was his shoulders and the back of his neck.

A moment later he straightened, looking self-satisfied. "Got it. Let me show you where it is, so you can light it again if it goes out," he said, gesturing for her to join him on the floor.

She hesitated, then did as he asked.

"It's way in the back on the left, see?" he said, pointing with the flashlight.

"Where?" He was much too near. He smelled of soap and freshly laundered cotton. She even caught the faint scent of cedar, from the lumber he'd been handling. "Oh, yes, I see," she lied, then promptly backed away. She stood and wiped her damp palms on the front of her khaki shorts. "Thank you so much,

Alex. And for fixing the balcony and fire escape—that's really above and beyond the call of duty."

"I'll expect payment," he said, his voice a lazy drawl as his eyes flicked over her, then danced away to focus on the flour sitting on the counter. "Cake?" he asked hopefully.

"Cookies," she said, relieved. "I'll bring some to you when they're done."

When he'd returned to his task on the balcony, she again sank into a chair and rolled her eyes heavenward. She could almost hear Chester laughing.

"Are they ready yet?" Emily asked a few minutes later, when the mouth-watering scent of oatmeal and cinnamon permeated the whole apartment and pulled her away from her beloved Saturday morning cartoons.

"You're just in time," Stacey replied, testing one of the cookies with her finger to make sure it wasn't too hot. "Would you like one or two?"

"How 'bout three?"

"One or two?" Stacey repeated.

"Three! Three, three, three, I want three," Emily insisted.

Stacey raised her eyebrows. "How about none?"

"Okay, two," the child quickly agreed. "Can I have one for Chester? Chester wants one."

Stacey tensed at the sound of his name. "Emily, can't you call your imaginary friend something besides Chester?" she asked sharply.

Emily appeared bewildered. "But his name is Chester."

"He isn't real! You don't have a real friend named Chester, do you?" Stacey demanded.

Emily's eyes filled with tears and her lower lip trembled, but she made no reply.

What am I doing? Stacey berated herself. Emily was just a baby. She was supposed to have imaginary playmates. Stacey grabbed two cookies from the cooling rack and held them out. "Here. Take your cookies."

Emily stared up solemnly at her mother but made no move to accept the treat.

Resigned, Stacey added a third cookie to the ones she held out. "And one for Chester?"

That did the trick. Emily grinned and accepted her bribe. Then she whispered, "He is real, Mommy, and he drives a red car and he's gonna give me a kitten."

"Is that so?" She absently patted Emily's head before the girl dashed off again. She couldn't believe she'd just let her own daughter manipulate her so neatly.

Shaking off her strange mood, Stacey put a dozen cookies on a small plate and covered them with plastic wrap, intending to quietly leave them in Alex's kitchen.

Alex dumped a can of pork and beans into a saucepan and set it on the stove. His habitual meals of hot dogs, frozen pizzas and things out of cans had begun to bore him, especially since he could usually smell some delectable something-or-other cooking up at Stacey's place. But he hadn't yet worked up the nerve to invite himself to dinner.

Actually it wasn't a matter of nerve. Stacey would probably welcome the opportunity to cook for someone besides Emily, whose tastes ran to macaroni and cheese with ketchup.

Rather, it was something else that held him back, some indefinable worry nibbling at his subconscious. It wasn't just the sexual pull between them. He couldn't deny there was one, not after that kiss, and not after the way his body had responded to her when she'd hugged him at the top of the attic stairs. But Stacey was at least as cautious as he was in that area, and with the constant presence of their three-year-old chaperone, there wasn't much likelihood they would do anything foolish, like fall into bed.

Then what was he worried about? he wondered. What could be standing in the way of two healthy, single adults enjoying each other's company?

He thought of Jeanne, but she wasn't the answer. Not the whole answer, anyway.

He smelled something burning and realized he'd let the pork and beans scorch. He turned down the heat and stirred the blackened mess in the pan. It looked disgusting, he thought, cursing softly.

"Problem?"

He slammed the lid on the pot and turned down the heat even further. "Oh, hi, Stacey. No, no problem." He wouldn't mind if she cooked a meal for him now and then, but he didn't want her to volunteer out of pity. An otherwise competent thirty-year-old shouldn't be as lousy a cook as he was. "Are those my cookies?" he asked, directing his hopeful gaze toward the plate in her hands.

"Your reward, sir," she said, placing the plate on the counter with a royal flourish. "The oven works fine. How's your repair job coming?"

"Almost done. Then I'll just have to paint it."

"I can do that," she volunteered. "I'm not what you'd call handy, but I can wield a paintbrush. Er, how much does paint cost?"

He smiled and shook his head. "You spend too much time worrying. There's paint downstairs. In fact, there's enough to do the whole house, inside and out. Apparently Chester had a lot of improvements in mind that he never got around to."

"Oh, Chester!" She flopped down in a chair at the kitchen table. "If I hear his name one more time today I'm going to scream."

"You're not letting those silly notes get to you, are you?"

"It's not just the notes. It seems my daughter converses with your grandfather on a regular basis. They're fast becoming best friends."

Alex looked amused. "Really?"

"It's not funny. I mean it was sort of cute at first, but it's starting to give me the willies."

"Stacey! You can't mean to tell me you believe in ghosts."

"No," she answered quickly. "No, of course I don't. But he signs his notes with 'Yours always.' *Always*. Kind of makes you wonder what he had in mind. What kind of car did your grandfather drive, anyway?"

"What?" Alex asked, momentarily taken aback by the odd question. "Why?"

"Just humor me."

"The last car he had was a '76 Monte Carlo. Green."

"Whew! Thank goodness. What are you cooking?"

He didn't answer her question. A sudden memory popped into sharp focus, something he hadn't thought of in a long time. "When I was a kid, Chester had an old MG, a convertible. God how he loved that car. We used to wash and wax it every Sunday, and then take a drive in the country."

"What happened to it?" Stacey asked.

"Someone stole it. It was never recovered. Chester could've bought another one with the insurance money, but he couldn't bring himself to replace it. After that, he drove sensible American cars."

"Alex... what color was the MG?"

"A wicked candy-apple red," he answered with a mischievous grin.

Stacey groaned and lay her head down on the table. "That figures."

"What's wrong with red?"

She shook herself, then flashed him a falsely bright smile. "Nothing. Hey, how's Ramona doing?" Ramona had given birth to a seven-pound boy the previous Monday.

"She's home from the hospital and already bored silly. She says Raul sleeps all the time."

"Lucky for her. Emily cried twenty-four hours a day till she was six months old."

Alex smiled sympathetically, but his thoughts were bittersweet. Once he had actually looked forward to a day when he would awaken bleary-eyed for a two o'clock feeding, or walk the floor with a colicky baby.

"When do you think she'll be ready to start work for me?" Stacey asked.

"Yesterday," Alex replied.

"Good. I'll give her a call and set up some time next week to go over the—what's that funny smell?"

Alex belatedly realized he'd turned the heat up instead of down. The contents of the pan were smoking. Guiltily he shoved the whole saucepan into the sink and ran water over it. "Never mind. Have you had lunch?"

She shook her head. "But I'm not *that* hungry."

"What?" Then he laughed. "No, no, I mean, let's go out. Come on," he cajoled when she looked as if she might say no. "You've hardly set foot outside this house except to deliver your newsletters to the post office. I know, we can get deli sandwiches and have a picnic at the botanical gardens—you and me and Emily."

Her initial impulse was to say no, but darned if she could think of a reason to refuse. She'd never seen Alex quite so animated about anything, and in the end she couldn't find it in herself to disappoint him. "All right," she said. His answering smile carried enough wattage to light up the whole house, and she felt good about her decision as she thumped barefoot up the stairs.

Emily adored her "Uncle Alex" and was pleased to go anywhere with him, so she donned her socks and tennis shoes without a fuss and even allowed Stacey to wash her face. "Did we ever go on a picnic?" she asked as Stacey combed the child's hair and fastened it with a barrette.

"Come to think of it, I guess not," Stacey answered. "Run downstairs and tell Alex this will be your first picnic. And tell him I'll be down in just a minute." She waited until the sound of Emily's footsteps faded into silence, then stood in the middle of the living room and glanced around, feeling nervous and foolish at the same time.

"Well, Chester," she said aloud, "you're getting just what you wanted. Alex and I are living in the same house, and now we're going on a picnic together... I'll admit he's a nice guy, even if he is still hung up on his wife, and he's good with Emily."

He also makes me tingle and flutter from head to toe, she added silently.

"I'm going to give this thing a chance, honestly. So stop pushing me, okay? I've had enough of the notes. And how dare you promise Emily a kitten. I haven't decided that yet."

She waited, as if expecting to hear an answer, but the wind in the trees outside was all the answer she got. She shrugged. It hadn't hurt to try.

The weather was perfect for a picnic—sunny and breezy and warm but not hot. Armed with enough food to last them a week, they drove to the quaint botanical garden, just a few blocks from their own house. The tiny park was fashioned on the grounds of a beautiful old estate, one of Topeka's lesser-frequented attractions. So even on a perfect picnic day, Stacey, Alex and Emily found themselves almost alone as they walked along the trails through a miniature forest of every kind of tree imaginable.

It didn't take long to see everything, including a small rose garden. Then they found an inviting spot to spread out their quilt, under an ancient black oak. Some of its gnarled branches reached all the way to the ground.

"Emily, aren't you going to finish your lunch?" Alex asked solicitously a few minutes later. The little girl had taken only three small bites of her peanut-butter-and-banana sandwich.

"Not hungry," she said. "Can I go play?"

"Go ahead," Stacey answered. "But stay where I can see you."

Emily raced off with her soccer ball, one of her favorite toys, as Alex looked on disapprovingly.

"It's my fault she's not hungry," Stacey confessed. "I spoiled her lunch with cookies. Besides, this is her first picnic. I don't want to ruin it by nagging her."

Alex stretched out onto the spot Emily had vacated, leaning on one elbow. "I suppose you're right. What's your excuse?" He looked at Stacey's half-eaten ham-and-cheese.

"I'm saving room for that chocolate cheesecake," she said as she started to wrap up the leftovers. "You know, this really was a nice idea. Days like this are so rare, it's a shame to waste one. And it feels so good just to relax and do nothing." She leaned back on her elbows and closed her eyes, letting a patch of sun warm her face.

It did feel good, Alex agreed silently. Almost too good. How long had it been since he'd treated himself to such a simple pleasure? But the feelings roiling around inside him were far from simple, and he wasn't sure why he couldn't just relax and enjoy the afternoon, like Stacey.

He studied her unhurriedly, thinking not for the first time what a beautiful woman she was—inside and out. How could he have ever imagined her to be a gold digger? The dappled shadows played jealously over her body, as if daring Alex's hands to do the same, and the light breeze teased her hair. A strand of the auburn silk blew across her face. He found himself reaching for her, intending to tuck the errant lock behind her ear.

He stopped himself before he could touch her. That indefinable worry nibbled at him again. What was it that held him back?

He would have pondered the problem further, but a flash of red in the tree caught his eye. His heart came up in his throat as he realized the flash was Emily.

"Look at me, Mommy," she called out, just as Alex bolted upright in a dead panic.

Stacey's eyes flew open. "Oh, my word," she breathed. "How did she get up that high?"

"I'll get her," he said as he rose to **his** feet, but Stacey grabbed his arm.

"Don't scare her, for pity's sake. She's probably fine." Then in a louder voice, she said, "Emily, honey, you need to come down from there. That's too high for you to climb."

How could she remain so calm? Alex wondered, fighting the urge to scale the tree and pull the child to safety.

"But I like it up here," Emily argued.

"Right *now*," Stacey said in a tone that left no room for compromise.

Emily pulled a face but did as she was told, gradually working her way downward. Her foot slipped once and Alex couldn't breathe for a second or two, but she recovered herself and continued on, unconcerned.

As soon as she was within reach, Alex couldn't stand it anymore. In three giant steps he was at the base of the tree. He reached up and grabbed the child, clutching her briefly to his chest before setting her on the ground. But even then he didn't let her go.

"Don't you *ever* climb something that high again," he scolded. "You could fall and break your neck. You scared your mother and me half to death."

Emily trained her huge blue eyes at her mother for a moment. Stacey took one step forward, as if she might interfere, then seemed to change her mind. She halted and folded her arms.

Emily crossed her arms in direct imitation of her mother.

"Did you hear me, Emily?" Alex bellowed, giving her a small shake.

She promptly let out a blood-curdling shriek. Alex instinctively recoiled, and she ran to her mother, wailing all the way.

Stacey picked up her daughter and cuddled her without a word. Then she gave Alex a look, just a look, but it said more than any words could have. She'd looked at him the same way the night he'd called in Paul Gibbs.

The ride home was conducted in an uncomfortable silence. Emily, buckled into her car seat in back, snuffled dramatically all the way, and Stacey's jaw was set firmly, as if she were biting her tongue to keep from verbally tearing Alex limb from limb.

"I'm sorry, all right?" he said as they pulled up to the curb in front of the house. "I overreacted, but she almost gave me a heart attack."

"Emily's the one you should apologize to," Stacey said as she got out of the car. "You scared her a lot worse than she scared you."

Alex wasn't so sure about that. He still thought the kid had gotten exactly what she deserved. But since he wasn't her parent, it wasn't his place to discipline her. That's where he'd gone wrong.

Oh, hell—if it took an apology to restore harmony, he'd have to go through with it. "Emily?" he said cautiously as soon as they'd come inside.

She turned and looked at him solemnly, clutching her soccer ball with both arms.

He bent down until he was at her level. "I'm sorry I got so angry with you. I was scared that you would get hurt, that's all. I still like you. In fact, you're my favorite little girl. Did you know that?"

Emily stared down at her feet.

"Would a T-R-I-P to the Z-O-O be in order?" he asked Stacey.

She nodded stiffly.

"Emily, do you like animals?" In a matter of seconds the deal was struck. Emily gave her "Uncle Alex" a hug, assured him he was forgiven, then raced upstairs to tell all of her stuffed animals that she was going to visit their cousins tomorrow.

"How about you?" he asked Stacey when they were alone.

"The zoo? Oh, I suppose I could stand it," she said, leaning against the back of the living room sofa with mock aloofness.

"No, I mean, do you forgive me, too?" He came up beside her and put an arm around her waist. He couldn't bear to have her angry with him, he realized.

She started to pull away, then seemed to change her mind. "If Emily can, I guess I can, too. But Alex, don't yell at her like that. A firm word of caution was all that was needed. She's just a kid, and kids explore—it wasn't as if she was disobeying. No one ever told her not to climb the tree."

"I know all that," Alex said softly. "I just... panicked for a moment, that's all."

"I don't want her to grow up afraid of her own shadow."

"I'll try not to let it happen again," he said. "I just don't want to—" he stopped himself, shocked at what he was about to say.

"Don't want to what?" she prompted.

I don't want to lose her. But she wasn't his to lose, and he had no business thinking in those terms. "Nothing." He forced a smile. "We'll do hot dogs at the zoo, okay?"

Stacey held her stomach in mock protest. "I'm still trying to recover from today's lunch. Too many more of these family outings and I'll be as big as a hot-air balloon."

Family outings. The words hit Alex like a truckload of bricks. That's what had been bothering him about the time he spent with Stacey and Emily. It felt too much like a family whenever he was around them. They welcomed him too warmly, accepted him too readily. But they weren't *his* family. And he was hardly a family man.

He'd almost been one, once. But fate had taken that one chance away from him. The loss had almost killed him—killed him inside—and he'd sworn he'd never allow himself to hurt like that again.

He couldn't be hurt—as long as he didn't hope, or dream, or envision a future with anyone. He reminded himself of this as he watched Stacey climb the stairs.

Chapter Six

Dear Alex,

You were always itching to get your hands on this house—not out of greed, I know that—but so you could fix it up. Well, here's your chance. Everything you'll need is somewhere in this basement.

Let Stacey help you. If she's half the girl I think she is, she'll roll up her sleeves and go after any task that needs doing. And when you're all done, the two of you can admire what you've accomplished. Working toward a common goal draws people closer, you know.

Yours always,
Chester

Alex found the note under a can of paint in the basement. This was the first of Chester's messages addressed to him rather than Stacey, and he had to admit that it gave him a peculiar feeling. He was sure Chester had planned it this way—to create the impression that he was still around, watching over them.

Alex reread the note with a mixture of nostalgia and irritation. His grandfather had good intentions. But Alex resented the manipulation, particularly because it was working so well and there didn't seem to be a damn thing he could do about it. As before, he and Stacey had anticipated Chester's wishes. They'd been working together on the old house for the past three weeks, evenings and weekends.

They had found six massive wooden columns in a corner of the basement, beautifully carved and just the right size to replace the front porch's unsightly brick supports. They weren't the originals—those had succumbed to termites, Alex recalled. Chester had obviously salvaged these from some other house.

After the columns were in place, the house looked so much better that neither Alex nor Stacey could resist the idea of painting. So they'd scraped the peeling frame house for two weeks, replaced boards as needed. Today they were to begin the actual painting, and they had both gotten up this morning as excited as kids on Christmas. Stacey was at the hardware store now, buying a few extra supplies they would need.

Alex felt a pull on his pant leg. "Watcha readin'?" Emily asked.

"I thought I told you to wait for me upstairs," he scolded mildly. He was relieved to note that today, at least, she was wearing shoes. Like her mother, Emily had a habit of running everywhere barefooted. Now that the weather had warmed up, it was nearly impossible to keep shoes on the kid.

"You took too long," she rationalized. "Watcha readin'?"

"Just a letter from my grandfather," he replied, folding the paper and tucking it into his jeans pocket.

"Chester?" Her eyes lit up. "Whas he say?"

"He says we ought to get to work painting the house," Alex replied, giving her two brushes to carry. "You take these, and I'll get the paint—no, this way," he said when she started for the stairs. "We can go out the back door."

As they exited into the bright May sunshine, Alex almost tripped when something wrapped itself around his ankles. He regained his balance and looked down just as Emily shrieked in delight.

"My kitten! My kitten!" She dropped the brushes and tried to pull a small gray-and-white bundle of fur into her arms. Sharp little claws adhered to the leg of Alex's jeans for only a moment before the cat gave in and allowed Emily to cuddle it enthusiastically.

"Now where did that come from?" Alex wondered aloud.

"From Chester," Emily answered without hesitation. She plopped down on the grass and stroked the half-grown cat, which after an initial period of surprise seemed to enjoy itself. It rubbed up against Emily and begged for more attention.

The animal appeared to be healthy, if a trifle skinny, so Alex didn't see any harm in letting Emily play with it for a few minutes. It wore a collar, so it was obviously well taken care of.

Alex picked up the things Emily had dropped. "Come on, let's go. You can sit on the porch swing and play with the kitten until your mother gets back." Then Stacey could deal with telling Emily she couldn't keep her new friend.

The kitten followed Emily as if it were trained, around the house to the front porch. Emily climbed onto the porch swing and the cat jumped immediately into her lap.

Alex silently shook his head. This spelled trouble.

In the hardware store's parking lot, Stacey started her car's engine, unaccountably exasperated with Alex. She shouldn't feel that way—it wasn't fair—and yet she couldn't deny the emotion.

Her decrepit blue station wagon ran better than it had in years, thanks to the fact that he'd been tinkering with it. He claimed he'd only tuned it up and changed the oil and filters. He'd even allowed her to pay for the oil. But she had a feeling he'd replaced a few parts here and there without telling her, and the rear tires looked suspiciously newer than they had last week.

For the first time in her life she was on her own, providing a living for herself and her daughter. She loved the feeling of accomplishment it gave her, the freedom, the independence. And then there was Alex, trying to smother her with good intentions. That's where the exasperation came in.

It wasn't that she didn't appreciate his efforts. In fact, it was more than appreciation. The obvious evidence of his caring made her feel warm all over.

But sometimes he treated her like a fragile crystal figurine, instead of the strong woman she knew she could be. He worried over every little thing, from a headache to a stubbed toe, and if she'd let him, he would wrap her in cotton batting in an effort to protect her from all the evils of the world.

Sometimes his attitude toward Emily bothered her, too. Though he obviously adored her daughter, and the feeling was mutual, he didn't let an hour go by without cautioning her about some danger. "Don't run up and down the stairs, you might fall," he'd tell her at least once a day, when the child was as surefooted as a mountain goat. And once he'd caught her cutting up paper with Stacey's sewing scissors, instead of her own blunt-ended safety scissors, and had lectured her for ten minutes on the dangers of sharp things. He had installed extra smoke alarms all over the house and had even conducted a full-blown fire drill.

Stacey was afraid that Alex, with all his dire warnings of hazards lurking around every corner, would turn her gregarious daughter into a timid mouse. Already the word "dangerous" had become part of Emily's vocabulary.

But Stacey could hardly get angry with Alex. His heart was in the right place, after all, she kept telling herself. He *needed* to care for someone, as Chester had pointed out in the note she'd found yesterday, inside the kitchen light fixture when she'd changed the bulb. Alex had been alone for a long time, and the fact that he was finally reaching out to someone was making a difference in his life as well as hers. She could endure a lot if it was helping him to exorcise the ghosts of his past.

At any rate, she didn't want to jeopardize the growing closeness between them. During the time they spent together working on the old house, they had developed an easy camaraderie. They talked about everything in the world—everything but Alex's marriage, that is.

They laughed a lot, too, and they touched—oh, nothing quite as explosive as that one crazy kiss, which now seemed like years ago. But Alex frequently put a hand to her shoulder, or smoothed her hair away from her face, and she found herself straightening his collar, brushing flakes of paint from his chin, or even slipping an arm about his waist.

These frequent tastes of intimacy didn't leave either one of them unaffected. Sometimes Stacey fancied she could see a fire in Alex's eyes, the same fire that flickered to life inside her whenever she was near him. But he seemed to be holding back, as if he were afraid to get too close, to hold her. And for that reason, she remained cautious, too. It wasn't just the fact that Emily was in constant attendance.

She sighed as she pulled up in front of the old house. Thinking it to death wasn't going to bring her any answers. Sooner or later their mutual attraction would either follow its natural course or stagnate—the former, she hoped. But before they could move ahead, Alex would have to look back on his marriage, and on Jeanne's death, and put some things to rest.

All thoughts of Alex came to a screeching halt when Stacey spied her daughter sitting on the front porch fondling a kitten.

"Where did that come from?" she demanded as she climbed the porch steps.

Emily looked up, unperturbed. "From Chester," she replied matter-of-factly.

Stacey bit her lip to keep from screaming. She dropped the sack from the hardware store with a *thunk*. "Where's Alex?"

Emily pointed upward.

He was on the roof, painting the dormers. Stacey paused a moment to admire the beautiful charcoal gray color of the paint and then another moment to appreciate the handsome backside of the man applying the paint, before she remembered the cat. "Alex!"

He looked up from his work, then down at her, shading his eyes from the sun with his hand. "Oh, you're back. Did you find everything we needed?"

"Never mind that. What do you know about a certain feline-type critter that's taken up with my offspring?"

He smiled benignly. "His name is George."

"Alex Peyton, did you or did you not give my daughter a cat?"

"I did not. Chester did."

"That is *not* funny."

"Now, Stacey, don't blow a gasket," he said, laying his brush on the rim of the paint can. He climbed down the ladder, and she watched the faded denim of his jeans stretch and strain against his thighs. The pleasing sight blunted her anger.

"The cat just appeared a few minutes ago," he said when he reached the ground. "It was waiting outside the basement door. But it's wearing a collar, so it's not a stray. It'll wander on home soon enough."

"Oh. How do I explain that to her? She asks me every day when May fifteenth is."

"May fifteenth?" he repeated.

"That's the date I promised I would decide if she could have a kitten. She's not going to let me off the hook."

"Maybe you should get her one. She seems to be enjoying George." He nodded toward the porch, where Emily sat on the swing, clutching the kitten to her chest and singing to it. The cat bore a pained expression, but it was tolerating Emily just fine.

"I'd love to get her a pet," Stacey said wistfully. "I'm sure we could find a free kitten, too, but then there's the vet bills, and food and cat litter...and don't you even think about it," she said when she noticed a speculative gleam in Alex's eye.

"But look how happy she is."

Stacey couldn't argue that. Instead she tapped his chest with her index finger. "I'll tell you what I told her. May fifteenth. I'll decide then." Less than a week away. How did she get herself into these messes?

"The sun's getting hot," Alex said, changing the subject. "We'd better get busy with the painting."

"I just need to run inside and change clothes. Did you say you had a shirt I could wear? I can't find my old clothes. Haven't seen them since we moved."

"Sure. There's a blue shirt hanging on a bedpost in my room. A pen leaked all over the pocket, so it's definitely paint-smock material."

"Thanks. I'll be just a minute."

On the way inside she sat down on the porch swing with her daughter. As if on cue, the kitten abandoned Emily and climbed into Stacey's lap, purring and rubbing up against her. It was a handsome little thing, she had to admit, snow white with charcoal gray spots the same shade as the house was soon to be.

"George likes you, Mommy," Emily observed.

"I like George, too, but he can't stay," Stacey said, deciding not to beat around the bush.

Emily thrust out her lower lip. "He's my kitten."

"No, he isn't. He's wearing a collar, so he must belong to one of our neighbors."

Emily shook her head. "Chester gave him to me."

How could Stacey argue with such logic? "Emily, George belongs to another family. Right now there might be some other little girl, crying because her kitty is lost, so we have to send George home."

Emily seemed to consider this. "Okay," she finally said in a small voice. She'd never lacked for compassion. "Go home, George."

Stacey set the cat down on the porch. It looked around, then immediately jumped back up into Emily's lap, appearing only a little less pleased than Emily herself.

"I give up," Stacey muttered as she headed inside.

The shirt was exactly where Alex had said it would be, hanging on his bedpost. It had obviously just come back from an unsuccessful stint at the dry cleaners. A dark blue splotch marred the pocket.

He should have let her try washing it, she mused. With Emily around, Stacey had learned how to eradicate every manner of stain. Now it was too late—the ink was set for good.

She slipped the shirt on over her white tank top, pausing a moment to savor the clean smell of starched cotton. The scent reminded her of Alex. She rolled the sleeves up several times, then tied the tails at her waist.

She glanced in the dresser mirror, to see just how ridiculous she looked, but the framed photo of Jeanne snagged her attention. The woman was such a mystery. What had she been like? Had her marriage to Alex been a happy one? How had she died? If only the smiling photo could talk. Somehow, Stacey felt that if she knew more about Jeanne, she would understand a lot of things about Alex.

But he was such a private man. He hadn't mentioned his wife's name since the fateful night of the spaghetti sauce, and Stacey had never summoned the courage to ask him about her. She felt she was prying just by looking at Jeanne's photo.

She turned to leave, but another picture caught her eye, a frameless snapshot tucked into the edge of the mirror. It showed a graying Chester behind the wheel of a red convertible, a dark-headed little boy in the passenger seat. They were both grinning ear to ear.

"That explains one thing," Stacey murmured. Alex must have shown the photo to Emily, and that's how the child had known that Chester once drove a red car.

By the time she returned outside, Alex had made short work of the attic dormers and was progressing downward from the roofline. Stacey opened a fresh can of paint and started painting from the foundation up.

She soon discovered it was satisfying work, this transformation. Hard as it was to believe, the white elephant was taming down and turning into a beautiful house. Once the painting was done, all it lacked would be a new roof. Then they could start on the inside.

"Hey, Stacey," Alex called down to her, later in the afternoon. They'd been talking all day, about everything under the sun, and the conversation had relieved the monotony of painting. "How's Ramona doing?" he asked. "I haven't talked to her lately."

Stacey froze. She'd known this question would come up sooner or later and had been dreading it for days. "Alex, I...I had to let her go." She resumed painting at a furious pace.

He said nothing for a few moments. Then, "Why?"

"Because she wasn't doing the job. She seemed enthusiastic at first, and her qualifications were so good I just turned all the advertising over to her, but she didn't follow through."

"What, exactly, didn't she do?" Alex asked sharply as he again climbed down the ladder.

"I had four separate advertisers call me last week, complaining that she hadn't returned their calls or sent them information they requested," Stacey explained as she continued to paint. "And it seems she had a shouting match with my biggest account. Now their advertising manager is so mad he's pulling out of a six-month contract. Ramona did apologize—it seems she'd been up all night with the baby and she was on a short fuse. But we both agreed that it just wasn't working out. We parted on good terms."

"Then you really fired her?" Alex asked, still incredulous.

Stacey laid down her brush. "I'm sorry. I know she's your friend, but—"

"Please, don't apologize. I'm the one to blame."

Had she heard him right? "You?"

"I never should have suggested you hire Ramona in the first place, but she was a first-rate account executive when she worked for me. I can't believe she would actually argue with a client."

"It's not her fault," Stacey said, quick to defend Ramona. "Motherhood does strange things to your life—believe me, I know..."

But Alex wasn't listening. "I feel terrible about this. Will the loss of the advertising revenue hurt you badly?"

"Well, not too badly," Stacey hedged. "But all I can do is pick up the pieces and go on."

"Who's the client?" Alex asked suddenly. "Maybe I could talk to him, explain what happened—"

"Don't be ridiculous! It's not your problem."

"Yes it is. I never should have interfered."

"Alex, all you did was introduce me to Ramona. It was my decision to hire her. So, she didn't work out. I'll find someone else. It was a good idea, hiring a salesperson. I just have to find the right one."

"I'll compensate you for the lost income," he continued, like he hadn't heard a word she'd said.

"No," she replied firmly. "I appreciate your concern, but it's misplaced."

"Maybe I could find an account to replace the one you lost," he continued, as if she'd never spoken.

This was getting out of hand. Stacey grasped Alex by his upper arms, gaining his full attention. "Alex, listen to me. You've given me a lot of help and advice over the past few weeks, and I appreciate it, but my newsletter is not your responsibility. Ramona's job performance has nothing to do with you. It's *not your fault*. So drop it. Okay?"

He appeared unconvinced, but nonetheless he nodded his agreement. She released her hold on him, only then realizing how tight her grip had been.

"You want some lemonade?" he asked, the subject of Ramona seemingly forgotten. "I have a pitcher made up in the refrigerator."

Stacey was relieved he'd backed off. "Sounds divine. I'll go get it."

He halted her with a hand on her arm. "No, I'll get it. I need to make a phone call, anyway."

She watched him go, thinking what a strange encounter that had been. How could he *possibly* believe that he was responsible for what Ramona had done? Then again, she shouldn't be surprised. Alex Peyton would bear the whole world on his shoulders if someone would let him. He'd already taken her little family under his wing, and now he considered the house renovations his concern, too. How could she possibly feel like a responsible adult, in control of her own life, when he was around? And yet how could she tell him to back off, when he wanted so badly to take care of her and Emily?

She would have fallen down on her knees in gratitude if Rich had displayed even a fraction of the concern she got from Alex. But there had to be a happy medium.

Thoughts of her ex-husband brought a sour, metallic taste to the back of her tongue. She'd spent three years trying to make that self-absorbed man happy—three years putting her own needs aside in favor of his. Three years of tip-toeing around him, trying to anticipate his moods and his wishes, until she'd become virtually a nonperson. She'd had very little identity apart from him.

And what had that gotten her in the end? Nothing she did had satisfied him. He'd left her pregnant and disillusioned.

It had taken her years to regain her self-confidence, to believe in herself again. And yet here she was, putting her own need for independence aside, letting Alex coddle her because she liked to see him smile.

But really, she was being too hard on herself. Hadn't she just stood up to him? She'd been firm, and he didn't seem to be taking it too hard. She took a deep breath and stood back to admire her work.

She needed the smallest brush to work around the intricate window frame. Last time she'd seen it, Alex was using it.

She peeked through the kitchen window and saw that he was still on the phone. Maybe she'd just climb up to the roof and see if she could locate the brush.

She eyed the sixty-foot aluminum ladder with trepidation. She'd never climbed such a tall ladder before, but it appeared to be sturdy and well anchored. With a shrug she began the ascent, one slow step at a time.

This wasn't so bad, she mused as she reached the roofline. She spied the brush she needed immediately and retrieved it, then set about climbing back down. But the moment her foot hit the first rung, she experienced the oddest sensation in the pit of her stomach, as if she wasn't sure which way was down. She glanced over her shoulder, just to get her bearings, but that only increased the sensation. Then suddenly she was dizzy.

She clamped her eyes shut and clung to the top of the ladder with one foot still on the edge of the roof. Good Lord, she'd never experienced vertigo in her life. But she sure had it now. She opened one eye. So far, so good. But when she looked down to find her footing, everything spun. She closed it again, positive she was destined to tumble to her death.

This was preposterous! But she couldn't talk herself out of it. She was virtually paralyzed.

"Alex?" she called out. But he was still inside. And Emily, who'd finally been persuaded to let go of the kitten for long enough to take a nap, was probably sound asleep in her bedroom.

"Alex!" she called again, louder this time. She heard the front door slam and breathed a small sigh of relief. Her white knight was on the way.

"Stacey? What are you doing up there?"

"I'm... I'm sort of stuck," she said in a thready voice. "I climbed up here just fine, but then I got dizzy—"

"Hold on, I'm coming to get you."

"No, really, if you'd just hold the ladder..." But she felt the ladder give under his weight and knew her feeble protest would be ignored. In truth, she was glad he was coming to get her. She felt like an idiot, but she was too scared to care.

In moment he was behind her, the hard security of his chest a welcome brace against her back, his arms on either side of her. "I've got you, honey," he said softly. "You're all right, you won't fall." His breath warmed the back of her neck.

For a minute she just let the welcome relief wash over her.

"Take your time," he said. The soothing tone of his voice calmed her skittering pulse. She was actually breathing. "Why don't you put both feet on the ladder?"

She did, moving her foot off the roof one slow inch at a time.

"Now, take one step down. You'll have to let go of the top of the ladder, honey."

She realized her hands were in a cramping grip against the sharp aluminum. She loosened them, slid them down the sides of the ladder a few inches, then took one shaky step down. After another step, this one more sure, she opened her eyes. The vertigo was gone.

"I'm okay, now," she said.

"Yeah, right," he said under his breath, making no effort to move away from her. Even when they reached solid ground, he didn't give her any breathing room. Instead he swiveled her to face him and wrapped both arms around her, hugging her so tightly she thought her bones would crack. But she could feel him trembling, too, and she knew that some powerful emotion had swept over him.

"It's all right," she soothed, just as he'd comforted her moments ago.

"God, you scared me. What were you doing up there?"

She tried to ignore the censure in his voice. "I wanted that little paintbrush to use around the trim, and I—"

He didn't even let her finish her explanation. "You should have called me," he said as he stroked her hair. "You have no business climbing that high."

"Alex, that tone of voice didn't work with Emily and it won't work with me. I'm an adult, and I'll make my own decisions about where I climb."

"You just did, and look what happened! What if I hadn't come along when I did?"

"Then I would have pulled myself together and gotten down that ladder, somehow," she said, though in reality she probably would have stayed up there until the next ice age. But if she gave in to his ridiculous argument, she'd find herself agreeing to get his permission before she crossed the street. "You're being an alarmist. Nothing happened."

"But it could have, damn it. You have to be more careful, Stacey. I couldn't bear it . . ." He didn't finish the sentence. He didn't have to.

The argument was over. His overprotectiveness might border on domineering, but Stacey knew he cared for her. He really did. And he was afraid that something might happen to her. She realized it at that moment, and she was filled with a warm, glowing light and then a *zap* of awareness that took her by surprise.

It's just the adrenaline, she told herself. But whatever its source, the passion was suddenly there, in her and in him. He tipped her head back and pressed his lips against hers, and because it felt so natural, she was neither surprised nor displeased.

He kissed her as if she were made of delicate porcelain. "I won't break," she whispered. Then she reached up and laced her fingers in his hair, guiding his mouth firmly back to hers. He tasted like lemonade and smelled like paint and hard work. And he was warm. The fear had chilled her, and now she sought that warmth the way a dog seeks the hearth in winter.

He pulled away so abruptly it made her gasp in shock. He turned his back on her, obviously struggling for some kind of control.

"Alex?" She was suddenly more afraid than she had been on top of that ladder. "Alex, what's wrong?"

"Nothing," he mumbled. "It's nothing. I'm sorry, Stacey—"

"Sorry, hell!" She moved around him until she faced him again. "You can't tell me 'nothing.' It's Jeanne, isn't it? You feel as if you're betraying her?"

He shook his head. "It's not that," he said tightly.

"Then why don't you ever talk about her? Why don't you ever share your memories of her, instead of keeping it all inside you as if you were a...a burial vault?"

Alex flinched visibly, and Stacey immediately regretted the harsh words.

But she couldn't let it go. "You can't tell me it's none of my business. You just made it my business, because whatever the hell it is that's eating away at you, it's driving me crazy."

"Then I'll tell you what it is," he said vehemently. "I wish you'd never come here. I don't need a surrogate family, and I don't want to care about you or anyone."

Her first instinct was to flee. How could he say something so hurtful to her? How could he be so cruel? But his last few words penetrated the pain. He'd said he didn't *want* to care... She took a chance. "But you do care, don't you?"

For a moment his eyes blazed denial, and she started to turn away, but then he dropped his chin in defeat. "Yes."

With that single word she was in his arms again.

"Oh, Stacey, don't leave me, not yet," he whispered fiercely, crushing her to him. "Someday you can, I promise, but I'm not strong enough now."

She felt hot tears pressing against her eyelids. "You're stronger than you know, Alex," she said. "You've come this far. You'll make it the rest of the way."

Chapter Seven

"I've never seen a cat so completely devoted to a human being," Alex commented late one afternoon, two weeks later. He and Stacey sat on the porch swing, watching Emily and George play in the front yard. "That kitten follows her around like a lovesick puppy. I thought cats were supposed to be independent."

"So did I," Stacey replied lazily, leaning her head on Alex's shoulder. She had one leg drawn up, a glass of iced tea resting against her knee.

She had tried to ignore George, hoping he would go away, but the cat was always either on the back balcony or the front porch. She'd taken him around to dozens of people up and down the street, but no one recognized him. She'd put an ad in the paper and had even taken a picture of him and made posters to hang around the neighborhood, but no one claimed him. And meanwhile, Alex was feeding the cat. He never admitted it, but Stacey could smell tuna on George's breath.

By May fifteenth no rightful owner had come forward, so Stacey declared that the cat belonged to Emily. They took him to the vet, bought him a flea collar, and brought him into the house with much pomp and circumstance. Now Emily and George were inseparable.

Alex and Stacey had become pretty inseparable, too, a circumstance that both thrilled and worried Stacey. She'd broken through part of the wall that guarded Alex's heart that day he'd pulled her off the roof. He had opened up to her, to the point that he had even mentioned Jeanne a couple of times, just in passing. Eventually he would tell Stacey about his wife's death, too—she was pretty sure of that.

What concerned Stacey was his ever-increasing protectiveness toward her and Emily, and her own reaction to it. He worried when either one of them was out of his sight, even for a minute. He called her every day from work, sometimes two or three times, just to "see how things are going." He fretted whenever Stacey took it upon herself to perform any type of strenuous task, like rearranging furniture or even lifting heavy bags of groceries.

She loved the fact that he seemed to treasure her, but did he have to take it so far? He made her feel helpless and even a little stupid sometimes, and that was one thing she couldn't allow to happen. She'd worked too hard to prove to the world and herself that she was strong and capable.

His attitude toward her business was a little disturbing, too. He'd sent three new advertising clients her way, a gesture she normally would have welcomed. But he acted as if he had a debt to repay her. No matter what she said, he still felt responsible for Ramona's disastrous stint as an employee, and he was trying to make it up to her in the most infuriating, bullheaded manner.

The problem was, it was damn near impossible to thwart Alex when he got an idea into his head. He did everything for her with such a generous, willing spirit, and with such obvious affection, that Stacey's objections seemed ungrateful. And in those instances when she did prevail and overrule him, he looked at her with sad, lost eyes that almost brought her to tears.

Rich used to do the same thing, she remembered, on the rare occasions when she went against his wishes. Only Rich had deliberately manipulated her with such emotions. It wasn't the same thing with Alex, not at all. She had to keep that in mind as she treaded the thin line between pleasing him and maintaining her own independence.

"What are we cooking for dinner?" Alex asked.

She closed her eyes and sighed. She didn't want to think about dinner, not yet. She liked it here, nestled in the hollow of his shoulder. "Beef stroganoff," she finally answered.

"Really? Are you sure I'm up to that?"

"It's not complicated," she assured him, "not for an old pro like you. Last week's meat loaf was a crashing success."

"Only because you coached me every step of the way. It would be less work for you if you just did the cooking yourself."

"No way!" she said on a laugh. "It's high time you learned. You were pathetic, eating out of a can every night. At least this way, you'll be able to fend for yourself when I'm not around."

"Where are you going?" he asked with an unmistakable note of alarm.

Good heavens, she'd only made a casual comment. She hadn't meant anything by it. But as long as he'd opened the door, this was as good a time as any to fill him in on her plans. "Actually, I'm going to see my mother next weekend. I'm really overdue for a visit. I'm sure she's grateful not to have me and Emily underfoot all the time, but she's not used to living alone."

"Oh." He paused. "You'll be gone all weekend?"

"From Friday afternoon till Sunday, probably."

"Oh," he said again. Then, "You won't be hitting Kansas City during rush hour, will you?"

"No, I won't leave here till after five o'clock. I have some appointments that afternoon."

"Then you'll be driving after dark," he said with distinct disapproval.

"No, I won't. These days it doesn't get dark till late."

"I have an idea. Why don't you let me drive you?"

"No, I don't think so," she said, gently but firmly. "I'm perfectly capable of making an hour-and-a-half drive."

"But that old car of yours—"

"Is in top running condition, thanks to you."

"What if you have a flat tire?"

"I know how to change a tire."

"But—"

"Alex!" She swiveled around and looked him in the eye, then took both his hands in hers. "I appreciate your concern, but please, give it a rest. I am not mentally or physically impaired. We're talking about a little jaunt to Kansas City to visit my mother, not a cross-country road rally."

He looked down at their clasped hands, then back up. "I worry about you, that's all."

She wanted to shake him and hug him all at the same time. She settled for a light kiss on the cheek. "You worry way too much. Come on, let's get dinner started."

The stroganoff was delicious, Alex thought two hours later, though Emily had drowned hers with ketchup and George flatly refused to taste the small portion Alex put in his bowl.

"You've spoiled that cat rotten with tuna fish," said Stacey as she put the leftovers in Alex's refrigerator.

"Me? I've never fed him tuna," Alex replied with exaggerated innocence.

"I suppose next you'll tell me Chester did it."

"Wouldn't surprise me. Hey, you haven't found any of his little notes lately, have you?"

"No—thank heavens," she added under her breath.

"Me either. Maybe we've unearthed all of them."

"Or maybe he's decided to give us a break, since we're falling in with his plans." She sounded at least half serious.

"Ah, yes, the matchmaking scheme." Alex stroked his chin thoughtfully. "Do you think this is what he had in mind? Sharing dinner a couple of times a week? Sitting on the porch swing watching Emily? Painting and wallpapering and sanding together?"

"I think it's exactly what he had in mind," she replied airily as she went to the sink to start the soapy water.

Privately, Alex disagreed. Chester never did anything halfway. If he'd chosen Stacey and Alex for each other, then he intended for them to marry and live happily ever after.

The old man most definitely had *not* intended for Alex to take Stacey to his bed without benefit of marriage. Yet that was exactly what Alex had on his mind this evening. He wanted Stacey—had wanted her almost from the first day he'd known her. Not so long ago, he'd thought that such intimacy between them would be a foolish move. He didn't think so now.

He had grown so close to her. He'd never thought he could share so much with any woman again. He'd tried not to care about her, but he did and there wasn't a damn thing he could do about it. So nothing stood in the way of their making love, provided Stacey felt the same way he did.

"Mommy, look at George!"

Nothing except Emily, Alex amended as he and Stacey both stared at the spectacle before them. Emily had clothed her kitten in one of her doll dresses. Poor George wore a long-suffering expression, but he shouldered the humiliation with dignity.

After drawing the expected laughter from her audience, Emily trundled off with George in her arms. Alex made a mental note to give the cat an extra helping of tuna for being such a sport.

He returned his attention to Stacey's back. She had her hair pulled into a ponytail, revealing the long, creamy length of her neck. Her shoulder blades were clearly discernible through the thin cotton of her blouse, and he considered them for a long moment. He'd never realized that shoulder blades could be sexy. His gaze wandered lower, past her slim waist to the pleasing curves of her hips. Then there were her legs—how could such a petite woman have such long legs?

He approached her quietly from behind, then slipped his arms around her waist and pressed his chest against her back. Though she constantly reminded him that she was strong and tough as shoe leather, she felt small and fragile in his arms.

He placed a soft kiss at her nape. He'd never done this before, had never caressed her so blatantly, and with such premeditation. So it might have been sheer surprise that caused Stacey's pulse to leap beneath his lips and her breathing to come in quick, shallow gasps. But he hoped not. It was time—high time—that he let her know how very much he desired her, and how precious she was to him.

"Do you realize we've never spent any time alone, just the two of us?" he asked, running the tip of his tongue along the edge of her ear.

Stacey turned off the tap and reached for the dishcloth to dry her hands. "No, we haven't."

"Doesn't Emily ever spend the night at a little friend's house?" he asked.

Stacey turned in his arms to face him. He was sure he knew what she was going to say, judging from her expression. *It's too soon. I'm not ready. You're not ready. We'd be crazy to...* Anything but what she actually said, which was, "Emily sleeps like a rock."

He thought he must have misunderstood. "What?"

"From nine at night until seven in the morning. She never wakes up, not for anything."

"Are you saying what I think you're saying?"

She nodded with a shaky smile. "If you're asking what I think you're asking. Oh, Alex, for so long I've wanted to... what I mean is, I didn't want to push for something that—oh, shut me up before I spoil it!"

He put an end to conversation in the most pleasing way possible. This was the only time he didn't worry about her—when she was tucked tightly in his arms, where he could see her, feel her life's breath mingling with his, smell the scent of sunshine in her hair. Nothing could happen to her as long as he was there to protect her.

Stacey reveled in the feel of his arms around her. At other times when he'd held her, she'd felt secure, sheltered. Now she experienced a delicious thrill of danger coursing through her as his hands roamed her body, warming her flesh with a bold caress here, a tender stroke there. His mouth was hard and demanding against hers, so that she could not mistake his intent. He wanted to possess her. She wanted to be his.

She let her fingers sift through his thick, soft hair. No man had ever made her feel this way, like she was walking a tightrope, on the verge of plunging downward with no safety net in sight.

She had hoped that Alex would come to this eventually, that he would see her not as a usurper trying to replace Jeanne, but simply as a woman who desired him, cared for him and wanted a place in his life. She hadn't expected him to arrive at this stage so soon. But here they were, and nothing had ever felt more right.

The sound of breaking glass in the living room yanked them both back to reality. Rising passion turned quickly to concern as they released each other and raced in the direction of the noise.

Emily stood by the fireplace, crying silent tears as she stared down at a pile of broken glass at her feet. Chester's photo had fallen from the mantel onto the marble hearth.

"George did it!" Emily said on a sob. "He jumped up there and—"

"Don't move, the glass is sharp," Alex interrupted. He was careful not to raise his voice this time, Stacey noted. "And you stay where you are," he said to Stacey, looking down pointedly at her bare feet. In the blink of an eye he'd scooped Emily into his arms, away from danger, and handed her to Stacey.

Emily buried her head against her mother's neck and snuffled.

"It's all right, pumpkin," Stacey soothed. "It was just an accident. We'll clean up the glass and everything will be fine. No harm done."

"I'll take care of it," Alex said, then added, "Don't you two ever wear shoes?"

Stacey didn't answer his question. "I think we'll go upstairs and have our baths," she said mildly. "Emily, thank Alex for dinner."

"Thank you," the child mumbled, her face still hidden.

"You're entirely welcome. See you tomorrow, ladybug." He kissed her on the top of her head, then returned his attention to the mess. He bent down to retrieve the wooden frame and picked off the last few fragments of glass clinging to it. "And you, Stacey—will I see you tomorrow? Or sooner?"

They both stared at the portrait in Alex's hands.

"Maybe he doesn't approve," Stacey said in a small voice.

Alex gave a nervous laugh. "That's ridiculous and you know it...but the same thought crossed my mind. You realize we're letting a phantom manipulate us?"

She matched his laugh. "Pretty silly. I'll, uh...I'll be down in a while." She turned and fled up the stairs before she could change her mind.

She gave Emily a bubble bath and chattered through it almost as much as Emily did. Once she had her daughter into pajamas and tucked into bed, with a penitent George curled up on the pillow next to her, Stacey attended to her own bath, using the scented oils her mother had given her for Christmas last year, the ones she'd never opened, but even the warm, fragrant water didn't cure her jitters.

She pulled the plug, blotted herself dry, dusted herself with powder, and went to ponder the lingerie drawer. She had no idea what would please Alex—nothing seemed appropriate. She considered a daring black silk teddy, then discarded the idea. It was a gift, also, but it really wasn't her style. Finally she settled on a demure cream-colored, floor-length gown with a matching robe. Then she brushed her hair until it shone. Her cheeks were pink from her bath, her eyes shiny with excitement. Would he find her attractive?

She ignored the doubts that had crept up on her. What had felt so right in the kitchen a few minutes ago couldn't possibly be wrong now. But she couldn't get over the way that picture of Chester had fallen and interrupted their mood.

She was just nervous, she told herself sternly. After all, it had been four years since she'd been intimate with a man.

As ready as she could be, she checked Emily to make sure the girl slept. She left the bedroom door open, as well as the front door to her apartment. If by some bizarre stroke of fate Emily did wake up, crying or calling for her mother, Stacey would hear her. But as she padded down the attic stairs, her thoughts were all for Alex.

The first floor was dark, but a light shone from Alex's bedroom. Stacey's heart hammered inside her chest as she drew closer to the half-open door. If she entered that room, there would be no turning back, no changing her mind.

She paused in front of the door. Should she knock? Or should she just float in and go to him, without words?

A movement caught her eye. Through the opening she could see Alex in the dresser mirror. He sat on the bed, still fully clothed, with a moody expression on his face and a mother-of-pearl picture frame in his hands.

Oh, God. Stacey backed away from the door before he could see her, then leaned against the wall, afraid that her knees would buckle and send her sprawling to the floor. Alex had been staring at the picture of Jeanne.

Stacey couldn't make love to him now, not when his mind was filled with thoughts of another woman. He wasn't ready for this step, she realized. Physically he desired her, but emotionally he was still tied to the past. His relationship with Jeanne was not yet a finished chapter. Until he was ready to turn the page, he couldn't give Stacey the unqualified love she craved.

Love. Was that what she wanted from him? She was perilously close to being in love with him, she admitted. To fall the rest of the way would be a very dangerous thing to do. What if he never came to terms with his ghosts from the past?

She couldn't just sneak back upstairs. Then Alex would think that she'd changed her mind for other reasons, that she really didn't want him. That wouldn't do.

She braced herself, then knocked loudly on the door.

There was a long pause. She heard the bed creak as he rose, heard a drawer open, then close. The thought of Jeanne's pretty smile being hidden in a drawer was disturbing.

Slowly Alex opened the door. His gaze seemed to drink her in. "You look beautiful," he said, but when he went to touch her, she held up a hand to stop him.

"Alex, we have to talk. I don't think this was such a good idea."

He didn't disagree with her, which only made her sadder. "What's wrong?" he finally said.

"I don't think either one of us is quite ready for this step," she said, and they were some of the most difficult words she'd ever spoken. "I have Emily to think about. She's very perceptive, and no matter how discreet we are, she'll sense the change between us. I don't want to confuse her."

"And if not for Emily?" he said, reaching up to stroke a lock of her hair.

She didn't stop him from touching her this time. "Maybe I'm not quite ready, either. You understand me well enough by now to know that I don't take this sort of thing lightly—"

"No one's taking this lightly," he said.

"I didn't mean that you were," she said quickly. "I just think we both need a little more time."

He sighed, then gave her a resigned smile. "All right. But if you were coming down here to dash my expectations to bits, you should have worn something besides silk." He touched the lace collar of her robe, then let his hand slide down her sleeve. He took one of her hands and pressed his lips against the back of it in a courtly gesture that squeezed her heart. Then he kissed her on the cheek, and closed his eyes.

She left before he opened them again.

Alex quietly closed the door and walked back to the bed, still a little shaky from the force of his desire. Yet he was almost relieved Stacey had changed her mind. He wanted her, and yet he'd known the time wasn't right. Hadn't he deliberately summoned up memories of Jeanne just minutes ago, hoping to find the strength he would need to send Stacey back to her own bed?

He wasn't sure what had prompted Stacey's change of heart, but he knew it was for the best. Crossing over the line of intimacy would change things irrevocably, and he wasn't ready for the commitment that implied. If she hadn't retreated, he probably would have, although he couldn't honestly be sure. She'd looked so beautiful, standing in the half-light of the doorway, almost like an angel.

Another time, he vowed silently. She would be his when the time was right, and not a moment sooner. He could only hope that he would recognize the right time when it came around.

Stacey checked the contents of her suitcase one last time before latching it. In it was everything she and Emily would need for the weekend. She glanced at her watch—ten minutes till five.

She had no real reason to hurry. There were hours of daylight left, and her mother wasn't expecting them any particular time. Yet Stacey felt an inexplicable urgency.

"Come on, Emily, it's time to go. Tell George goodbye."

"Why can't George come with us?" Emily asked. She sat on the living room floor, entertaining her kitten with a piece of yarn.

"Because cats make Grammy sneeze, remember? Now get Purple Teddy and your soccer ball and let's go."

Emily reluctantly did as she was told, dragging her feet all the way. When a roll of thunder rumbled in the distance, she paused and listened. "Ooh, Mommy, the angels are bowling!" she said excitedly. "Is it gonna rain?"

"Probably. That's why we should get going—to beat the storm."

"Is Uncle Alex coming with us?"

"No, not this time." And that's why Stacey was in such a hurry, she realized. She wanted to get on the road before Alex got home. He would make a fuss about them driving to Kansas City in the rain, and she'd just as soon not deal with his overprotectiveness at the moment.

She would miss him, though, even for the short time they would be apart. He had become a very important part of her daily life, and Emily's, too.

With the suitcase and a bag of toys for Emily in hand, she lumbered down the stairs toward the front door. In the living room, she felt compelled to pause. Something wasn't quite right.... Then she saw it— Jeanne's picture. It stood on the mantel, next to Chester's.

She put her things down and moved closer, to study it. Why had Alex put it there? She stared at it so long and so hard she never even heard the front door open, never realized Alex had arrived home until she heard Emily's excited, "Uncle Alex!"

By the time Stacey whirled around, a decidedly guilty flush to her face, Emily had jumped into Alex's arms.

"Hi, ladybug," he said, kissing the child on the cheek. Then he set her down and in two long strides had reached Stacey. He kissed her on the cheek, too. "I see you noticed the picture."

She nodded mutely.

"I couldn't bear to put it away," he said softly. "It didn't seem fair to just shut her away in some dark closet—"

"And I wouldn't want you to," Stacey added.

"But I figured it was time to move her picture out of my bedroom. What do you think?" he asked earnestly, as if her answer were very important to him. "Should it stay there? Would you mind?"

"Of course I don't mind," she answered without hesitation. In fact, now that he'd explained it, she thought it was an extraordinarily healthy and promising move on his part.

"Are you coming with us to Grammy's house?" Emily asked Alex.

"I don't think anyone's going anywhere tonight," he answered cheerfully, though Stacey detected an underlying strain beneath his smile. "Have you heard the weather report?"

"Nooooo," she replied, stretching out the word. What was he up to?

"We're under a tornado watch."

"So what? This time of year, Topeka is under a tornado watch every other day. They never amount to anything."

"This one might. There's a bank of awful-looking black clouds in the southwest." As if to underscore his observation, another roll of thunder rumbled in the distance.

"But it's not even raining yet. And I'll be driving east—I'm sure I'll outrun the weather, if we leave right away."

"I don't think you should take the risk. What if you run into hail? Or a flash flood? Or even a tornado?"

Was she imagining things, or had Alex's forehead grown shiny with perspiration? She shook her head to clear it of unexpected cobwebs. "Hail couldn't hurt my old car, and the Interstate isn't likely to experience a flash flood. Anyway, if the weather starts to get bad, I'll stop at the first place I see and wait it out. Now, I'd love to chitchat all night, but we really have to go."

"You can't."

She must have misunderstood. "I beg your pardon?"

"I said you can't drive to Kansas City with the weather so threatening. It's not safe."

Stacey balled her hands into fists. But before she could let her temper get the best of her, she noticed Emily, watching the two of them like a ping-pong game. "Emily, I forgot the, uh, bubble bath. Would you run upstairs and get it for me, please?"

The child gave her mother a look that said she wasn't buying this ploy, not for a minute. But she must have sensed Stacey's determination, because she sighed elaborately and then stomped away and up the stairs.

Stacey hated what she was about to say. She really did. But in this instance, she would have to stand up for her rights, even if it meant making Alex angry. "Now listen carefully, Alex," she said in a low, steady voice as soon as Emily was out of earshot. "Whether I stay or go is not your decision to make. Are we clear on that point?"

"Perfectly. You're still not going."

"You're being unreasonable."

"No, *you're* being unreasonable. There's no reason to take an unnecessary risk. You can drive to Kansas City just as easily in the morning."

"My mother expects us tonight. She's cooking a special dinner— Why am I even arguing with you?" she said, exasperated, as she picked up her suitcase and the toy bag. "I'm putting these things in my car. As soon as Emily comes back down, we're leaving. I'm sorry if that makes you uncomfortable, but you'll just have to live with it."

He followed her outside, dogging her steps, but had obviously run out of arguments for the moment.

She tried not to look at him as she opened the back of her station wagon and threw the suitcase inside. If he gave her that sad, whipped-puppy look, she would be tempted to cave in to his wishes. And if she did, it might restore immediate harmony, but in the long run it would spell disaster for their relationship. She would forever be a slave to this overbearing, unreasonable side of him, and she couldn't tolerate that.

She slammed the tailgate shut and reached to retrieve her keys from the lock, but they weren't there. She looked down at the pavement, thinking they must have fallen, then felt her jeans pockets, but the keys weren't there, either. Then she looked up at Alex, and she knew a moment of real panic.

"Give me back my keys," she said.

"No. I'm sorry, Stacey."

"I will not be treated like some disobedient teenager. Now give me my car keys."

"You can have them back tomorrow."

Why was he doing this to her? she wondered as she followed him numbly back into the house. Didn't he know what was at stake here? It wasn't just her trip to Kansas City. It was their whole future. If he wasn't willing to negotiate, or at least discuss his reasons for behaving like a Neanderthal, then they had no future.

She had to try one more time. "Alex, why?"

His words were barely a whisper. "Because I don't want to lose you."

"I'm afraid you've already lost me." With that she turned and retreated up the stairs.

Chapter Eight

Since Alex had treated her like a disobedient teenager, Stacey could think of nothing better to do than act like one. She ran into her bedroom and fell in a sobbing heap on the bed, crying tears of fury and frustration. She would probably scare Emily to death—she'd never become hysterical in front of her daughter. But tonight she was beyond control.

True to form, Emily wasn't scared. But she was curious and a little confused. "Are you sad, Mommy?" she asked.

Stacey pulled her daughter into her arms, taking comfort from the warm, squirming body and the little-girl smell of her. "Yes, I'm very sad," she said when she found her voice.

"Why?"

Because I feel like my life is crumbling around me? "Because Alex and I are angry with each other."

"Were you bad and he got mad and yelled at you?"

"Not exactly. It's different with grown-ups."

George picked that moment to jump up on the bed, not content to let the humans keep the hugs to themselves.

"George doesn't want you to be sad," Emily said, using the same strategy Stacey often used on her.

"George understands that sometimes grown-ups cry, too, but only for a little while," Stacey said, still fighting the sobs that came from deep inside her. She stroked the kitten's soft fur as he rubbed up against her and purred. "Then they start to feel better and everything gets back to normal." *In a million years or so.*

"Chester doesn't want you to feel sad," Emily said, sounding a little more anxious. "He told me so."

Chester? Stacey thought with a snort of disgust. If he hadn't meddled in hers and Alex's affairs, she wouldn't be in this mess in the first place. But she didn't suppose Emily needed to hear that. Stacey pulled herself together, for her daughter's sake. "You tell Chester that I'm feeling better already."

Emily seemed reassured.

Somehow Stacey made it through the evening. She called her mother and told her the trip had been postponed until tomorrow, due to the weather. She fixed dinner, though she couldn't manage even a bite of it herself; she played a game with Emily, bathed her and got her put to bed; she watched an old movie on television.

When it came to putting herself to bed, however, it was a hopeless case. Sleep was as elusive as a unicorn.

Stacey tossed and turned, steamed and fretted, and cried some more. It wasn't until after four in the morning that she finally dropped off, and even then, her sleep was fitful.

She was not prepared for the knock that rudely awakened her at seven a.m. She quickly pulled on a robe and stumbled to the door, feeling grouchy and gritty-eyed. The sight of Alex standing on the landing, a bouquet of daisies in one hand and her keys dangling from the other, did little to improve her mood.

She considered slamming the door in his face, but that would only prove to him that she was the child he tried to make of her. Besides, she wasn't angry anymore—just resigned, and sort of empty inside. She opened the door to admit him, making no move for either the flowers or the keys.

She gestured for him to take a chair in the living room, and she sat down in the other. He laid the daisies and the keys on the coffee table.

"I'm sorry," he said simply.

"I'm sure you are," she responded, her exhaustion making it almost impossible for her to deal with her own emotions, much less Alex's. "But if you were faced with the same situation, you'd do the exact same thing again."

He didn't deny the accusation.

"I'm not mad at you, Alex," she said with a sigh. "I know you didn't do it out of spite, or due to some deep-seated need to control me. You did it because you were worried, pure and simple. But your concern is out of proportion. I can't live with it anymore."

"What do you mean?" The question was laced with raw fear, which only made Stacey's next words that much more difficult.

"I'm leaving for Kansas City as soon as I can get myself and Emily dressed. When I get there, I'll ask my mother if we can move back."

"Stacey, wait a minute—"

"You're smothering me, Alex. I've worked so hard to get to the point where I could take care of myself and Emily, and you're taking that away from me. I thought I could deal with it, but every time I stand up to you, you get upset and you make me feel awful. I spent my entire marriage feeling awful because I couldn't make my husband happy. I won't put myself through that again."

"But you can't just... What about the house?"

"Consider it yours. Just pay the taxes and utilities, and in three years when it's free of the trust, I'll sign it over to you."

He pressed his mouth into a grim line. "We can talk when you get back. There's no need to make any hasty decisions."

"No, I don't think so," she said with absolute finality.

He opened his mouth as if to argue further, then seemed to think better of it. Instead he turned and exited, slamming the door behind him. She could hear his angry footfalls all the way down two flights of stairs, and she caught herself thinking, *Good*. Immediately she was ashamed of the childish satisfaction she'd taken from his anger.

As she and Emily were heading out of the apartment a little while later, Stacey spied the forgotten daisies lying on the coffee table. She quickly put them in a glass of water before leaving.

Alex watched through the living room window as Stacey and Emily climbed into the old blue station wagon. He'd blown it, big time, and he knew it. On one level he deeply regretted what he'd done. He'd driven Stacey right out of his life. But on another level, he knew that, just as Stacey had said, if he were faced with the same situation he would do exactly the same thing. When it came to protecting his own, he would not be thwarted.

He was a bit shocked to realize that he thought of Stacey and Emily as "his own." But he did. He loved them both, and keeping them safe from harm had become a priority in his life.

Still, his efforts had never yielded such disastrous results. On a number of occasions in the past he had been admittedly pushy in his quest to protect them. Stacey had reacted by either grinning and bearing it or firmly putting him in his place.

Last night was different. Maybe he *had* gone too far. Maybe his fears, exaggerated by the circumstances, had caused him to go a bit beyond the bounds of reason. A bit? "Hell, why don't you face it, man," he grumbled to himself. "You went berserk."

The situation yesterday had tossed him into a nightmarish déjà vu, reminding him of another evening when the weather was bad, and another woman determined to get into her car and drive to another town. Alex had let Jeanne go with only token resistance. He had trusted his sensible wife's judgment. If only he'd kept her home, she would have lived.

That thought had pounded through his brain last night, blocking out all other reason. If he could just keep Stacey and Emily from leaving, they would live.

Perhaps if Stacey understood *why* he'd panicked—but then, he'd never explained it to her. The night of Jeanne's death was something he never discussed, with anyone.

Never.

It wasn't fair for Stacey to be the one to move out, Alex decided as he slumped resignedly into the blue wingback chair. Chester had bequeathed the house to her, after all, and she had worked as hard as Alex on the renovations.

He forced himself to look around the room. The transformation that had taken place in the few short weeks he'd lived here with Stacey were nothing short of amazing. The walls had been patched and painted in soothing shades of eggshell and the palest peach—Stacey's choices. Everywhere he looked were her little touches: a needlepoint pillow on the sofa, a vase of dried flowers on the coffee table, a painting from a flea market hanging over the fireplace.

She'd turned this place from a house back into a home. He couldn't allow her to move out. If anyone had to leave, it ought to be him.

Never mind the fact that he loved her; he was making her miserable. She deserved a mate who would soar with her instead of always trying to pin her wings.

He could take his old apartment back. It was still vacant—he knew because apparently there had been a slump in the market and the manager had been trying to hold him to the broken lease.

The decision made, he launched himself into the task of packing. It kept his mind and body occupied, prevented him from dwelling on the terrible reality of separation.

He would leave most of the furniture, he decided. He didn't need a houseful of old stuff, didn't have room for it, anyway. He would take only the personal effects and a few of the books and knickknacks that held sentimental value.

And the living room rug.

Ever since the first time Emily had spilled something on the valuable Oriental carpet, Stacey had been begging Alex to roll it up and put it in storage.

He slid all of the furniture off the rug and began the laborious task of rolling it up into a tight column. How would he ever fit the thing into his car? he wondered as he struggled with the uncooperative carpet.

When he had it about halfway folded, he uncovered something curious—a manila envelope, taped to the hardwood floor. It had his name on it, as well as Stacey's.

"Oh, Chester, what now?" he muttered.

His grandfather's matchmaking shenanigans were the last thing Alex wanted to contend with at the moment. But the curiosity was unbearable—he had to open the envelope and see what was inside. His hands shook as he ripped off the tape and pulled out the single sheet of typing paper. Something else dropped out, too, clattering to the floor. A key.

He took a deep breath and began to read the spidery handwriting:

Dear Alex & Stacey:
No more games; I'm going to reveal exactly what my intentions were.

"It's about time, you old badger," Alex said aloud. He took another breath and continued.

First you, Stacey. When your mother decided to move with you to Kansas City to make a fresh start, I gave her my blessing. But we stayed in touch, through letters and telephone calls. She often sent snapshots of you, and I watched fondly as you grew from toddler to teenager to adult.

But it wasn't until Betty started sending me copies of your newsletter that I realized you would be the perfect match for my grandson—smart, compassionate, nurturing, and not unfamiliar with loss and hardship. I learned a lot about you from your monthly column—your love for cooking, your favorite colors. And from your mother, I knew of your need for a stable home life and a man who would cherish you, respect you and accept your daughter as his own. I'm afraid I used what I knew of you to shamelessly manipulate you into Alex's life.

Incidentally, did you try the spaghetti sauce? It was one of Alex's favorite dishes.

There's one idea that backfired, Alex thought with a bittersweet grin as he remembered the fiasco of the first meal Stacey had prepared for him.

As for you, Alex, I know how much you love this house, and I never intended to permanently cheat you out of your birthright. But a house is no compensation for a bitter, sterile existence, which is exactly what you were living. I knew that if anyone could do it, Stacey could bring you back to life and help you deal with the past. I wanted you to have both her and the house.

Apparently I was wrong. You wouldn't have found this note if you weren't moving out the furnishings.

Please believe that I love you, Alex, and I want only the best for you, Stacey. You're probably both angry with me for meddling in your lives, but perhaps the contents of the safe-deposit box will help restore your opinion of me.

I hope you both find what you're looking for.... Goodbye.

Yours always,
Chester

The last few words blurred. Alex was surprised to find a film of tears in his eyes. So, the old man had loved him after all. He'd never said so before, and Alex was just now realizing how important that was to him. And Chester had finally said goodbye. There hadn't been the chance before.

Helluva guy, Alex thought. Though his grandfather's methods were bizarre, they were motivated by love and the best intentions. His plan had almost worked, too. Almost. Damn.

Alex picked up the key and studied it. According to the small label attached, it would open a safe-deposit box at the bank where Chester had kept his accounts. The bank was less than a mile away. Alex couldn't resist curiosity's lure; he had to know the last piece of the puzzle, his grandfather's final gesture.

Abandoning his packing for now, he stuffed the key into his pocket and headed for the front door.

The ring of his phone stopped him. He hesitated, not really wanting to answer it. He was not in the mood to talk to anyone right now. He stood rooted to the floor as it rang five times; six, seven. Then it stopped.

He was almost out the door when it started ringing again.

"Damned nuisance," he muttered as he strode back through the living room and to the kitchen. He yanked the receiver to his ear. "Yes?" he said curtly.

"Alex?"

"Stacey?" His lungs constricted for a moment and his pulse all but stopped. Something was wrong, horribly wrong. He'd heard the agony of her voice, though she'd spoken only the two syllables of his name. "Stacey, what's going on?" he said when she didn't respond.

"Alex, you have to come..." The rest of her words were choked off with tears.

He fought the panic that tried to invade his body and steal his wits. "Where are you?" he demanded. "Answer me, honey. I can't help you if I can't find you."

"P-police station. On Massachusetts," she managed.

"In Lawrence? What happened?" He braced himself for her answer, clutching the edge of the kitchen counter in a white-knuckle grip.

When she spoke again, her words were calm, detached, as if that was the only way she could get them out. "It's Emily. She's missing. Please come—I need you, Alex."

He didn't hesitate. "I'm leaving right now."

He made the drive to Lawrence in a record twenty minutes, but each of those minutes dragged into an eternity. Emily, missing. How? Had she been snatched out of Stacey's car at a stoplight? Or had she simply wandered off at a gas station or restaurant? Was she hurt? Scared? The possibilities were terrifying, and they twisted Alex's gut into such a knot he had trouble staying on the road.

Thank God he knew exactly where the police station was, so he didn't have to waste time asking directions. In the parking lot, he jumped out of the car almost before he'd shut off the engine, then sprinted into the low, beige brick station house, unmindful of the curious stares people directed his way.

He spotted Stacey immediately, slumped into an orange vinyl chair in a corner of the waiting room. She looked as small and fragile as he'd ever seen her, her face pale as plaster, her hair mussed, as if she'd been dragging her fingers through it. The mere sight of her was enough to make his throat constrict; the unquestioning welcome he saw in her eyes did him in completely.

In the span of a heartbeat she was out of the chair and in his arms, crying hot tears against his shoulder. He held her tightly, as if his own body could absorb some of her pain and fear.

"Easy, honey, easy," he soothed, stroking her hair and gently rubbing the tense muscles of her back. He wished he could tell her that everything would be all right, but he was reluctant to make meaningless promises. He needed to know what the situation was.

She clung to him with childlike trust as he dampened his handkerchief at the drinking fountain, then bathed her flushed face with the cool water. He guided her back to her chair and brought her a cup of coffee. After a few minutes, Stacey got herself under control, enough that she could tell Alex what had happened.

"I didn't get much sleep last night," she began, punctuating each sentence with a sigh and a sip of coffee. "On the way to Kansas City I found myself nodding off at the wheel. I pulled into a rest stop, thinking it would help if I got out of the car and stretched my legs, maybe got a drink of water.

"Emily was asleep in her car seat. Rather than wake her up, I locked all the doors and then ran up to the shelter house, where the drinking fountain was. I knew I wasn't supposed to do that—you should never leave a child in a locked car—"

"Stacey, it's all right. Don't worry about that now." But Alex had a feeling she wouldn't take that advice.

"I was gone less than a minute," she continued. Her voice rose at the remembered panic. "I ran the whole way, thinking that would wake me up. When I got back, the car door was standing wide open and she was gone. I looked everywhere. She just...vanished."

"Do you have any idea what happened?" he asked, struggling to keep his own voice calm. He refused to heap his own anxiety on top of Stacey's.

"The police think Emily opened the door herself. There's no sign of someone breaking in. She must have gone looking for me, then climbed back into the wrong car. Or she might have been lured out—" Stacey's voice broke.

"Oh, Stacey." He folded her into his arms again, causing her to spill her now-cool coffee on him. He didn't care. "Don't cry, honey. It'll be fine. I'm sure she's fine. It's just a mistake, that's all. The police will find her any minute." He said the words, whether he really believed them or not, because it was what she needed to hear. She was on the edge of hysteria. She needed hope to cling to.

"Why did I leave her?" Stacey asked, her voice muffled against Alex's shoulder. "I knew better. If only I'd taken her with me..."

"Don't do this to yourself," he said sternly. He recognized the all-too-familiar threads of guilt and regret in her words. "Don't punish yourself this way. You can't blame yourself..."

The sentence trailed off as a strange realization struck him. The words he'd just spoken weren't his own. He'd borrowed them from his grandfather. How often had Chester uttered the same sentiments in an effort to release Alex from the guilt of Jeanne's death? And how often had Alex rejected the comfort his grandfather had tried to give, preferring instead to wrap himself in his cocoon of guilt?

He'd lived with that crippling guilt every day of the five years since the accident. He couldn't allow Stacey to do the same thing to herself, to suffer years for one instant of inattention.

"What's wrong?" Stacey asked, momentarily distracted from her own distress by the strange look on Alex's face. His whole body had grown suddenly tense, and he stared off into the distance as if watching the approach of something vitally significant. She shook his arm when he didn't respond. "Alex?"

Abruptly he turned that searing intensity on her, and she saw something more than concern for her daughter in his pain-filled eyes. "This might seem like a hell of a time to bring this up," he said with quiet determination, "but I have to tell you something. I have to tell you about Jeanne."

Chapter Nine

Stacey held her breath. She'd waited a long time for this confession, and she wanted to hear it, no matter how awkward Alex's timing. She wasn't sure what had prompted it, but she did know that the only way he could hope to find happiness was to deal honestly with his loss, instead of holding it to him like a security blanket.

At least if she focused her attention on Alex, it would keep her from dwelling on her missing child. Maybe talking about Jeanne would distract Stacey enough from the endless, agonizing waiting that she could hold on to her sanity a little longer.

"I need some fresh air," she said quietly. "Let's walk outside for a minute, and I'll listen to whatever you want to tell me." She signaled to the desk sergeant that she would be nearby, in case there was any news, and then they exited through the double glass doors.

Hot, bright sunshine and a gentle breeze made a refreshing change from fluorescent lights and stale air-conditioning. Alex and Stacey found a small patch of grass in the dubious shade of a stunted tree and settled onto summer-warmed ground, close but not touching each other.

It was a long time before Alex spoke, and when he did, he kept his eyes trained into the distance. "She died in a car accident."

Inwardly, Stacey cringed. She'd guessed that Jeanne's death had been sudden, but that didn't make the reality any less tragic.

"It was in the winter, shortly after Christmas," Alex continued, then paused and swallowed. "We were supposed to drive to Wichita for the weekend, to visit some friends. But I had an emergency come up at work that couldn't wait until Monday. Jeanne decided to go ahead anyway, and I was supposed to join her when I could get away." He paused again, longer this time.

Stacey was compelled to fill the silence. "Then you weren't with her when—"

"I should have been," he said, the words coming out like a scratched record, as if he'd already said them a couple of million times. Maybe he had. But almost immediately the sharpness left his face, and his posture lost its ramrod straightness. "Ah, hell, I don't know anymore. The roads were starting to ice up, but she was determined to go. She had four-wheel drive and new tires, and she was a very good driver. I let her leave without a whimper."

"And what happened?" Stacey prompted.

"The car skidded off a bridge and into a swollen creek. By the time I was notified and got to the hospital, she was gone. So was the baby."

Stacey felt as if she'd been punched in the stomach. *Baby?*

"Jeanne was pregnant," he clarified.

"Oh, Alex..." She took his hand and squeezed it, hard. How horrible it must have been for him, then and also last night when she'd unwittingly forced him to relive the nightmare. "No wonder you were so set against my leaving. The situation was so similar—why didn't you tell me then?"

He still wouldn't meet her gaze. "I should have, I suppose," he said gruffly. "But it's not something I normally talk about."

"Then why now?"

He looked at her then, his eyes blazing intensely once again. "Because I have to make you understand something. All these years I've been blaming myself for Jeanne's death. I kept thinking, if only I'd gone with her, I could have prevented the accident. If only I'd kept her from leaving, she'd be alive today. If only we'd chosen another weekend to travel to see our friends—"

"But you can't blame yourself for what happened," Stacey objected.

"That's just it. I do. Or rather, I did...you've made me see something that Chester tried and tried to tell me. You can't hold yourself responsible for someone else's actions. And you're not responsible for plain rotten luck."

"Of course that's true for you, but my situation is entirely different," Stacey argued as she came crashing back to the present, back to her own circumstances. She clenched her hands into tight fists. "I shouldn't have left Emily in the car by herself."

"For a few seconds? Stacey, you didn't do anything that millions of parents haven't done. A kid can disappear anywhere, any time. It's just plain damn rotten luck. It wasn't your fault."

"But if I'd just—"

"Look, if you're going to blame someone, why not me?"

That brought her up short. "You?"

"I'm the one who upset you so badly last night that you couldn't sleep. If you'd gotten a good night's sleep, you wouldn't have pulled into the rest stop. I thought I was preventing a potential disaster, and instead I caused one. If I'd just let you leave when you wanted to, none of this would have happened."

She chewed on that thought for a few moments as she rubbed a blade of dry grass between her fingers. "You think you're to blame?"

"*No one* is to blame. Some things simply can't be predicted or avoided, no matter how careful you are."

She surprised herself by smiling, if only briefly. "But you still try, don't you?"

"A little too hard sometimes, I guess," he mumbled. "But try to understand what I'm saying. Don't make the same mistake I made. Don't saddle yourself with that guilt. You'll just make yourself sick with it, and it won't bring—" He cut himself off before completing the thought.

"It won't bring Emily back," Stacey finished for him in a wooden voice.

"They'll find her," he said firmly, clasping her hand between both of his.

When he said it with such conviction, she believed it. Without thinking much about it, she reached up and touched his face. "Thank you for telling me about Jeanne," she said. "I know it must have been hard. And I do see the point. But where do you draw the line? What if I'd left Emily in the car ten minutes instead of a few seconds? When does a person take responsibility?"

"All I know is that a guilt trip doesn't do anybody any good," he replied.

Responsibility. She repeated the word in her head as silence claimed them again. It had become a recurring theme in her life. How often had her mother tried to tell her that she couldn't hold herself responsible for Rich's happiness? Stacey had punished herself over and over, believing that if she'd just tried a little harder, been more patient, loved him a little more, the marriage would have worked. But it was Rich who was fundamentally unhappy, and nothing she could have done would have changed that.

If he couldn't find contentment with a devoted wife and the promise of a family, that was *his* shortcoming. She'd learned that lesson once. She'd also come very close to forgetting it, those times when she'd sacrificed her opinions and her good judgment in favor of Alex's, in a doomed attempt to make him happy.

Alex was the only one who could make Alex happy. He was the only one who could work through the tragic events of his past, and thank God he was taking steps in the right direction. She could offer support and encouragement—and love—but he would have to do the work himself.

She did love him. She couldn't fool herself about that any longer. As soon as she had her daughter back, she would have to deal with her feelings.

"Do you think you could..." Her voice broke. She tried again. "Do you think you could just hold me for a little while?"

Without hesitation he pulled her to him and wrapped strong arms around her, cradling her head under his chin. "Anything, honey. I'll do anything you want me to do."

And he did. During the next few hours he became Stacey's self-appointed slave and guardian. He brought her tea and coffee and a hot lunch, though she couldn't bring herself to eat. He read aloud to her from the police station's collection of dog-eared magazines, and rubbed her stiff neck and shoulders. He telephoned her apartment every few minutes, to see if anyone had left a message on her answering machine. He also called her mother from time to time, though there was precious little news to relate.

For once, Stacey didn't object to being coddled. She drew strength from Alex. His reassuring touch calmed her, and his mere presence kept her panic at bay. He had to be nearly as distraught as she; he was a worrier to the core. But he never let his fear take control of him. She admired him for that.

Later that afternoon, a tracking dog was brought in to search the rest stop and the surrounding terrain, where Emily had disappeared, but to no avail.

"If she were anywhere within miles of that rest stop, that dog would have found her," the young detective on the case informed Stacey. "We have to conclude that your daughter left in a car."

And so the search intensified. Stacey provided several photos of Emily, which were quickly copied and sent to area television stations, for broadcast on the evening news. That brought nothing but a few crank calls.

As daylight faded into dusk, there still was no word.

"Detective Morris wants me to take you home," Alex finally told Stacey. "He can get more done if he doesn't have to worry about you sitting out here. Why don't you let me take you to your mother's house?"

"No," Stacey said fiercely. The first twenty-four hours were crucial, Morris had said. Emily *would* be found before morning, and Stacey was determined to be on hand.

"You'll be just a phone call away," Alex tried again. "I'm sure Morris will keep you informed. And I know you and your mother would both feel better if you were together."

"Mom is probably beside herself," Stacey agreed, forcing herself to reconsider. She'd tried to talk to her mother, but every time Alex handed her the receiver, she ended up crying.

"She's worried, just like you are," Alex said. "Stacey, honey, you're exhausted. If you don't get something to eat and some rest, you aren't going to be much good to Emily when she does turn up."

Stacey sighed. "If I leave here, it'll feel like I'm giving up," she said in a small voice. "As long as I stay here, it seems like Emily could still be found just any moment..." She struggled to keep the tears at bay. She'd never been much for crying—had certainly never cried as much as she had during the last twenty-four hours, not even when Rich had walked out.

"Whatever would make you feel better," Alex said. "If you want to stay here all night, I'll stay with you."

At least he had left the decision up to her, Stacey thought with small comfort. Maybe there was hope for him yet. "Who will feed George?" she asked suddenly. "If anything happens to that cat, Emily will never get over it."

"George isn't in any danger of starving," Alex assured her. "If he gets hungry, he can catch that mouse you saw in your kitchen."

"Worthless beast," Stacey said under her breath. "Why would he catch mice when you keep feeding him tuna?" She'd been pacing, but now she sank into a chair, suddenly exhausted. Emily could be in another country by now. What did it matter if Stacey waited at a Lawrence police station or in Kansas City, with her mother? "You're right, Alex," she said, coming to an abrupt decision. "Let's give Detective Morris my mother's phone number, and we can go to her house and wait there."

"You want me to come with you, then?"

"Oh, yes, please," she said, clinging to his arm. "Please don't leave me. I don't want to be alone—not even for the time it takes to drive into the city."

It was just simple human companionship she wanted, then, Alex thought grimly as Stacey told the detective of their plans. She didn't want to be with Alex in particular. Any warm body would do. He would stay with her, of course—he would do anything to get her through this in one piece. But her attitude toward him apparently hadn't changed since this morning. When she and Emily were reunited, Stacey would have no more need for him.

Alex kept up a steady stream of meaningless conversation as they drove to Kansas City, a vain effort to distract Stacey. But he could hardly draw any response from her. She sat stiffly in the passenger seat, her fists clenched in her lap, speaking only when she had to give Alex directions.

Betty Kidd lived in a small but pretty stucco house in an older neighborhood near the Country Club Plaza district. The woman herself stood anxiously at the door, and as Alex pulled his car into her driveway, she stepped outside. Stacey flew out of the car and was immediately enveloped in her mother's arms.

He stood back for a moment to study Stacey's mother. She was an older version of Stacey, with the same intelligent blue eyes, but with sunny blond hair cut in a short, stylish cap. Her linen slacks and jacket showed a studious interest in conservation fashion, a marked contrast to her daughter's more casual taste in clothing.

Just when he thought the two of them would ignore him altogether, Stacey motioned for him to join them.

"Mom, this is—"

"Alex!" Betty interrupted, taking his arm as they headed indoors. "I'd know you anywhere. You look so much like Chester—well, like he did when he was younger."

Stacey headed directly for the phone in the hallway, to call the police station.

"How is she?" Betty asked in an undertone, guiding Alex to the living room.

"Not great. She hasn't eaten anything all day."

"She never could eat when she was worried or upset. I'll see what I can do. I put a casserole in the oven when you called—"

"You shouldn't have gone to the trouble," he objected.

"When *I'm* worried or upset, I cook. Let me get you something to drink. Lemonade? Iced tea? I have all manner of soft drinks—"

"Just some water, thanks." He didn't really want anything, but the woman obviously needed to keep herself busy. She was like a violin string, vibrating long after she should have gone still.

Before Betty could leave the kitchen, Stacey reentered the room, her face pale and grim. "Detective Morris is sending someone to the house in Topeka, to intercept any messages. He said to expect a pair of detectives here, too. Meanwhile, they said if anyone calls, we should keep them on the line, keep them talking..."

"Dear God, they don't actually think she was kidnapped!" Betty interjected.

"They think it might be Rich," Stacey said, again relying on that flat, emotionless voice. "Apparently kidnappers almost always turn out to be a relative, or a former spouse, and Rich is the only candidate. I told them it was a ridiculous notion—that if Rich had any interest in Emily he'd have expressed it before now. But they still suspect him because they haven't been able to locate him."

"Maybe they're right," Betty said thoughtfully. "It would be just like Rich to all of a sudden decide he wants to be a daddy, and then just take the child. If it *is* him, he'll realize soon enough how much trouble a three-year-old can be and he'll change his mind. You'll see."

"Better him than some stranger," Stacey said with a shiver.

The phone rang. All three of them jumped.

Stacey looked first at her mother, then at Alex. "You get it," she said.

He wasn't sure he wanted to take what might be a very important call. What if he said the wrong thing, something that endangered Emily? But seeing Stacey's trusting blue eyes locked on him, he suddenly felt equal to the task. He picked up the living room extension before it could shrill out a third ring.

"Kidd residence."

"Detective Morris," came the now-familiar dour voice. "May I speak with Ms. Kidd, please?"

Stacey pressed her lips together as she took the phone. "Yes?"

Alex resisted the urge to lean close and listen in. Instead he watched her face, studied it for some sign as to what information the detective relayed. It was something important, judging from the way she chewed on her thumbnail as she listened, but whether it was good or bad, Alex couldn't tell. She never said a word, except an occasional "uh huh."

After what seemed like an eternity, she hung up the phone. He could see now that her eyes were filled with tears, and some of the moisture slipped out as she tried, and failed, to speak.

"Stacey, honey, what is it?" Alex asked, inwardly terrified to hear her answer.

"They found her." Stacey took a deep breath and then smiled as her words began pouring out, one on top of the other. "She's safe, she's not hurt, and she wasn't kidnapped. As near as they can figure, there was a truck full of chickens parked near us at the rest stop. You know how Emily is about animals—"

Both Betty and Alex nodded.

"Anyway, she got out of the car and climbed onto the truck to get a closer look at the chickens, and the truck drove away with her in the back and the driver none the wiser."

"She *climbed* onto a *truck?*" Betty asked, horrified.

At the same time, Alex asked, "Where is she now?"

"Sedalia, Missouri. That's where the driver finally unloaded his cargo and found her. They didn't know what to do with her at first, and then I guess it took awhile for the various law enforcement agencies to compare notes and figure out who she was, and then—"

"Well, for heaven's sake, what are we doing standing around?" said Betty. "Let's go to Sedalia and get her!"

"No," Stacey objected. "They're bringing her here. She should be home in less than two...oh, dear." She put a hand to her forehead.

"What?" Alex and Betty said together.

"I don't feel so good."

Alex caught her just as her knees began to buckle. "Maybe if you wouldn't starve yourself," he scolded mildly as he guided her to the sofa, even though he himself felt weak with relief.

"I'll get you some milk, sweetheart, and some saltines," Betty said, making a hasty exit.

"She loves to fuss," Stacey said with a shaky smile.

Alex sank onto the sofa next to her. "You okay?"

"My little girl is safe. I couldn't be better." Abruptly, and quite unexpectedly, she threw her arms around Alex's neck and kissed his cheek. "Oh, Alex, thank you so much. I couldn't have gotten through this without you."

He reciprocated the hug with mixed feelings. He wanted more than gratitude from this woman. He loved her. And though she was warm and vibrant in his arms, already he could feel her slipping away again. By thanking him she was effectively dismissing him.

Betty reentered the room with a huge glass of milk in one hand and a plate in the other, but she immediately did a U-turn. "Oops."

"No, Mom, come back," Stacey called out as she and Alex sprang apart. "I need that food."

Betty returned, looking a bit embarrassed. "So I guess Chester's plan is working?" she asked hopefully as she set milk and some cheese and crackers on the coffee table. Stacey fell on it like the starving woman she was.

"What do you know about Chester's plan?" Alex asked casually.

Betty shrugged with what appeared to Alex to be exaggerated innocence. "Stacey's told me quite a bit."

"It was just a hug, Mom," Stacey objected. "Don't be picking out the china pattern."

Ouch. Twist the knife a little harder, Stacey, he thought, tossing her a look that told her just how hard her casual dismissal had hit. But she wouldn't meet his gaze.

Betty jumped up at the first opportunity to tend to her casserole, leaving Alex and Stacey alone, but somehow Alex simply couldn't find the right words to say. This wasn't a good time, anyway, not when Stacey was so focused on getting her daughter back. He would have to give her some space and time. She had accused him of smothering her, after all, so backing off was the least he could do.

The casserole turned out to be tuna, which Alex considered better suited to George than himself, but the two women took no notice of the fact that he pushed the food around on his plate without consuming any of it. They chatted nervously all through dinner, reminiscing about Emily's previous stunts, some of which would have turned Alex's hair white if he'd been around.

"Alex tried to tell me she was too fearless for her own good," Stacey said, nodding her head toward him. "I just thought he was being an alarmist. I guess I should have let him lecture her on safety more often."

Alex should have felt smug, but the only emotion he could muster at the moment was relief that he'd finally gotten his point across. Emily, brave child that she was, was not indestructible.

Stacey flew to the door when the bell rang a few minutes later. A grinning police officer stood on the front porch, holding a rumpled and drowsy Emily. "Did you lose something?" he asked as the grin widened.

"Mommy!" The child fairly flew from the officer's arms to her mother's.

Stacey clutched Emily to her briefly, then set her down so she could look at her closely. "Oh, baby, are you all right? I was so worried. Are you hungry? Are you... *what* is that *smell?*"

"I believe it has something to do with the chickens," the officer said helpfully. On that note he left.

For the next few minutes, there didn't seem to be enough of Emily to go around. She was passed from one set of arms to another like a doll, hugged and kissed despite her unusual aroma, and offered every manner of sweets. She appeared none the worse for her adventure. Apparently she'd enjoyed it.

"Didn't you even miss me?" Stacey finally asked, obviously exasperated.

"'Course I did, Mommy," Emily answered matter-of-factly. "Can we get a chicken?"

Stacey rolled her eyes. "Only if it's for the oven. Phew! Goodness, Emily, let's get you into a bubble bath. Give Grammy and Alex a kiss goodnight."

The child gave a dutiful round of hugs and kisses. When it was his turn, Alex squeezed her so tightly she squeaked in protest. This was probably the last time he would see her for a while, and he had to force himself to release her.

"Would you like some dessert, Alex?" Betty asked when they were alone. "I offered Emily everything under the sun and completely forgot about you. There's cherry pie."

"Ah, no, thanks, Mrs. Kidd. As a matter of fact, I need to be going. Will you be able to take Stacey to her car? It's at the police station in Lawrence."

"Well . . . sure, that's no problem. But why do you have to rush off?"

He couldn't tell her the real reason—that now that the crisis was over, he felt awkward and out of place. "I'm sure you and Stacey have a lot to catch up on, and I'd just be in the way," he said, settling for a partial truth. "I'll bring Stacey's suitcase in from the car and be on my way."

"Emily fell asleep almost before I could get her pajamas on," Stacey said, breezing into the kitchen where her mother was finishing up the dinner dishes. "Hey, where's Alex?"

"He went home," Betty said. "Or, more accurately, he escaped. I'd say it was the threat of my cherry pie," she quipped.

"Oh, no," Stacey groaned as her stomach fell. "He could have at least waited to say goodbye. I needed to talk to him."

"Oh? What about?" Betty asked casually, pouring herself a cup of coffee.

Stacey sighed. "There's just something I wanted to get straightened out," she answered evasively. "I promised myself I'd take care of it as soon as Emily was home."

Betty eyed her daughter speculatively. "Chester knew what he was doing, I think. Are you in love with Alex?" she asked point blank.

Stacey started to deny it, but there really wasn't any use. Her mother was too perceptive. "I suppose I am."

"And Alex has similar feelings?"

Stacey smiled at that. "I think so. No, I'm sure of it. He loves Emily, too."

"Then what's the problem?"

"The problem is that we had a terrible fight, and I told him I was moving out."

"Out of your own house?"

"It should have been his house, Mom. Anyway, I don't really want to move. I'm just not sure how to go about fixing things."

"'I'm sorry' and 'I love you' would make a good start," Betty said, nodding sagely. "But maybe it's better that he left tonight. You're both so exhausted from this ordeal with Emily, it might not be the best time for a serious discussion. You can rest and think things through, and then you can talk to Alex tomorrow when you go back."

Stacey nodded. "You're right. There's no hurry."

But she went to bed a few minutes later feeling anxious and edgy. By morning, she had convinced herself that there *was* a hurry. She felt an urgency, almost a compulsion, to return to Topeka as soon as possible.

Betty convinced her to stay through lunch, but by two o'clock Stacey was as restless as a caged tiger.

"I can take the hint," Betty finally said. "You're going to wear a rut into the floor if you keep up that pacing. I'll drive you to Lawrence to get your car."

"I'm sorry, Mom. It's not that I don't want to visit with you—"

Betty laughed. "Don't apologize. I don't blame you for being impatient to get back to Alex. Now go get your things."

Stacey didn't have to be asked twice. With a grateful smile she started for the bedroom, intending to hastily pack her clothes. But the sight of Emily's anxious expression halted her. "What's wrong, pumpkin?"

"I wanta stay with Grammy," she answered, her lower lip trembling.

"Why *don't* you leave Emily with me?" Betty said, obviously delighted with the prospect. "I can take some time off from work and spoil her rotten. Having her grandmother dote on her for a couple of days might be good for her at this point."

Leave Emily? Stacey was loath to even let the child out of her sight. But Betty had a good point. Although Emily had apparently suffered no ill effects from her recent adventure, right now she would probably benefit from an extra measure of safety, security and love. Stacey could hardly devote herself to properly pampering her daughter when she had her future with Alex hanging in the balance. And it would be undeniably easier for the adults to work out their problems without Emily underfoot.

"All right," Stacey finally agreed. Emily clapped her hands.

She said a tearful goodbye to both her mother and daughter in the Lawrence police station parking lot but then forced herself to get into her car and drive away. Her immediate objective—smoothing things over with Alex—would ultimately be for Emily's benefit, too, she reminded herself. Alex had become a strong, positive influence in the child's life, and she would be devastated if she lost him.

As she drove toward home, she wondered just exactly what she might say to Alex, the words she would use to convey her turbulent feelings. She had come to realize that her pride, her freedom and her independence wouldn't be worth much without him. Yet she ought to be able to have both his love and her pride.

She couldn't realistically expect him to change—his overprotectiveness had become an integral part of his nature. She would simply have to deal with it differently than she had in the past. Sometimes they would disagree, and she would have to stand up to him without feeling guilty. And perhaps she would have to give in sometimes—even when he was unreasonable.

Could she do that without undermining her own self-worth?

"Well, for heaven's sake, why not?" she asked herself aloud as she entered the Topeka city limits. Strong relationships were supposed to be built on compromise, on give and take. She and Alex would both have to try a little harder—that was all there was to it.

A wave of optimism washed over her as she drove down her street toward the house. Her faith in the future almost glowed.

As she pulled up in front of the house, she was relieved to see that Alex's car was parked at the curb. Now that she was fired up, she didn't want to postpone their confrontation. Climbing out of her car, she forced herself to assume a sedate pace as she made her way up the walkway and to the front door.

She started to call his name as she stepped inside, but the word stuck in her throat. The scene that met her hit her with the force of a ball bat to the stomach. The place was a wreck. Pictures were gone from the walls, the bookshelves were empty, and the rug was missing. She would have thought they'd been burglarized, except for the half-empty boxes standing around here and there.

Alex was packing up and moving out.

Chapter Ten

Alex himself stood in the middle of the living room. He locked gazes with Stacey, who had come to a screeching halt just inside the door.

"Hi," he said, running a nervous hand through his hair.

"Hi? That's it?" Stacey's words crackled through the warm air.

"I, uh, wasn't expecting you back so soon."

"Obviously. Sorry I spoiled your clean getaway. Mom referred to your leaving last night as an 'escape,' but I didn't take her seriously." She swallowed the lump that tried to form in her throat. She was absolutely done with the tears. Now she was ready to fight for what she wanted. "Just what the hell do you think you're doing? This is not what we agreed to."

"As I recall, we couldn't agree to much of anything," Alex retorted, meeting her anger lick for lick.

He turned away from her, and with one defiant sweep of his hand he collected the photos of Chester and Jeanne from the mantel and tucked them into a box. "You declared you were moving out, and that was that."

"And you decided to beat me to it."

"Why should you be the one to leave?" he countered. "The house belongs to you, after all."

"We're back to that argument, are we?"

Alex opened his mouth to retort, then closed it again with a puzzled expression. "Where's Emily?"

"Mom asked if she could keep her for a few days, and Emily liked the idea. Besides, you and I have some business to take care of, and I thought we could do it better without a chaperone."

"Is she all right?" he asked. "I mean, she didn't suffer any delayed reaction or anything, did she?"

Stacey tried not to let his obvious concern soften her. "If you were worried, why didn't you stick around to find out? You didn't even say goodbye."

"I wanted to get this over with," he said, gesturing with his hand. "I figured that if I cleared out before you got back, it would be easier on everyone."

"Easier?" Had she heard him right? "You were going to bug out like a thief in the night, knowing I'd come home to an empty house with no warning? And knowing that I can't afford to keep the house up by myself? How kind of you."

He didn't respond to her sarcasm. Instead he reached back into the box and retrieved the photos, then returned them to the mantel.

"You knew exactly how terrible I'd feel," she continued, "seeing the beautiful home we created together stripped of all its warmth. You wanted to hurt me. Just like... just like I hurt you." With those last words, the anger drained out of her. With a shudder of guilt, she thought back to how coldly she'd dismissed him from her life, how emotionlessly she'd informed him that there was nothing between them any longer.

She'd come home to make peace. Why was she arguing with him?

"Alex..." She moved swiftly across the room, feeling a need to physically connect with him. But he tensed when she touched his arm. "I'm sorry for the way I acted when I stormed out of here yesterday morning," she said. "I didn't mean any of those awful things I said, *especially* the part about moving out. I was angry and upset, and I struck out at you. I can't blame you for striking back. I didn't even thank you for the flowers."

He turned to look at her then, his brief flash of anger gone, too. For the first time she noticed the little stress lines around his hazel eyes. "So you came back intending to stay?" he asked cautiously.

"Yes."

"You said I was smothering you with my exaggerated and misplaced concern. Do you think anything's really changed?"

"Yes," she said again.

"How? We put aside our differences for a few hours because we were frightened half to death over Emily. Now that she's safe..." He shrugged. "I'm still the same hovering, overprotective guy, and you still want your independence."

She shook her head. "That may be true, but I've learned some things over the past couple of days, things about you, about myself—and about us—that make me believe we can work it out."

He studied her, as if gauging her sincerity. When he spoke, his words were surprisingly gentle. "What did you learn?" he asked, sinking onto the camelback sofa and pulling her down with him. He waited intently for her next words.

There would be no better time to take her mother's advice and tell him what was on her mind, she decided with a deep breath. "I learned why you're so cautious, why you worry so much. Understanding that will go a long way toward helping me to be more tolerant. But mostly I learned that I could be mad as hell at you, and still love you."

He greeted her admission with dead silence.

Her heart gave a panicky flutter. Why didn't he say something? But she'd gone this far. There was no turning back. "I do love you, Alex," she said, her words barely a whisper. "Does that surprise you? Scare you?" And when he still didn't respond, she added, "Horrify you?"

That drew a tentative smile from him, as if he wanted to believe her but didn't quite dare. He took her hand and absently rubbed her knuckles with his thumb. "It surprises me a little, I guess. I was looking forward to a long battle to win that prize, and here you've handed it to me wrapped in ribbons."

Now she was even more confused. "If you wanted my love, then why were you moving out?"

He looked around the room, as if seeing it for the first time. When he turned back to her, his expression was definitely sheepish. "You want to know the truth? When you walked in just now, I was putting everything back. Moving back *in*," he clarified. "I'd already decided that I was acting like a jerk by leaving you before you had a chance to leave me. Maybe I *was* trying to hurt you. Or maybe, in the back of my mind, I was hoping you'd miss me and come to appreciate my sterling qualities."

"But I already do," she argued, unable to stop herself from stroking his cheek. "And I don't want either one of us to move."

He sighed. "I'm not sure what's best anymore. The space and distance might be good for us. Maybe you need to really experience independence. That seems to be important to you."

She wanted to shake him in her frustration. She'd just admitted that she loved him, and he *still* was contemplating a separation? But he hadn't reciprocated, she reminded herself. He cared for her, but he was still wrestling with the hurts of his past.

"If you were to move out, Chester would roll over in his grave," she said, as a last resort. Maybe it was a low blow, bringing Alex's grandfather into the argument, but she was a desperate woman. How could they possibly work out their differences from separate houses?

"Chester!" Alex jumped up from the sofa as if he'd been bitten. "I forgot all about it. And the key." He patted all of his jeans pockets, coming up empty-handed.

"What key? What are you talking about?"

"I found another note, under the carpet. Now what did I do with it?" He made a brief search of the room, eventually zeroing in on one of the end tables. "Ah, here it is." He picked up a much-creased sheet of paper and handed it to her.

Stacey trembled as she read this latest message from Chester. It only confirmed what they'd figured out a long time ago, but the resigned tone of it made her heart feel leaden inside her chest. "I was right. He *is* disappointed," she said with a catch in her voice when she finished. "And it sounds so final, like we'll never hear from him again."

"Stacey, he's dead," Alex reminded her.

"I know. But sometimes it seems like he's here with us, and to tell you the truth I've gotten kind of used to that feeling. What's the safe-deposit box he talks about?"

"There was a key to a safe-deposit box with the note. I stuck it in my pocket and was on my way to the bank when you called yesterday. I forgot completely about it until just now."

"Where's the key?" she asked excitedly.

"I don't know where it is," Alex admitted. "I must have thrown those jeans in the wash—"

Stacey didn't wait for him to finish. She headed for the laundry room.

"Can't this wait?" Alex asked as he followed on her heels. "We were discussing something kind of important."

"You brought up the subject of the key," she reminded him. "Anyway, I have a feeling this might be important, too."

A telltale metallic clank punctuated the dryer's hum as it tumbled a load of laundry. Stacey opened the door and, after a brief foray into the warm clothes, her fingers touched on hot metal. "Aha!" She straightened, tossing the hot key from one hand to the other. "Alex, I think we'd better postpone any major decisions about who should move where until morning, when we can get into this box."

"What do you think is in there?" he asked.

She didn't say. But she highly suspected that the contents would change their lives. Judging from the way Chester had manipulated them so far, the wily old man's final gesture was bound to pack a wallop.

They were waiting at the front doors of the small branch bank when it opened the next morning.

"I hope you realize that I'm missing a very important business meeting for this," Alex commented as the security guard unlocked the door.

"Big sacrifice," Stacey said, trying to hide her jitters behind a teasing facade. "A team of wild woolly mammoths couldn't have kept you away from here. You're as curious as I am."

"And just as nervous, too." He took her trembling hand in his as they approached a bank officer. Soon they were being escorted to the vault, where a stern-looking trustee unlocked the box for them and then took them to a room where they could view the contents in private.

Once they were alone, they sat on opposite sides of the small table, the box between them, and stared at each other.

"Well?" Alex said.

"Well? Go ahead and open it."

"We don't have to, you know," he said. "We could pretend we never found the key."

"Sure. Now open it."

He shrugged and lifted the lid. They both leaned over the table and peered inside the box, the tops of their heads almost touching. Then Alex reached inside and pulled out a sheaf of papers.

"It's a copy of Chester's will," Stacey said.

"Not a copy," Alex corrected her. "A new will. And unless I miss my guess, it'll take precedence over the other one."

"Oh." She sank back into her chair, pondering the possible implications. "You read it. Tell me what it says."

"Sure you trust me?" he said with a wink.

"Just read it, Alex. The suspense is killing me."

"Okay, okay." He scanned the document, skipping over the preamble and the legalese, flipping through the pages until he got to the meat of the matter. He read the important part over twice, just to be sure, and then leaned back in his chair. "Oh, dear. You were right, this does change things."

"What?" Stacey demanded.

"He left the house to me." He waited, tensing in anticipation of her reaction.

She surprised him by smiling, then laughing aloud. "Thank God. It should have been yours anyway. I always thought I wanted my own house, but it's a tremendous responsibility. Maybe I wasn't quite ready for it...aren't you happy? Alex, you have your house back."

He shrugged. "A house is just a house," he said. "It's the people inside it that make it a home. There's more. Chester left you some money."

"Money? You're kidding. H-how...how much?"

"Enough that you can buy another house, if you want." He handed the document to her, pointing out the figure in question.

She gasped when she saw all the zeroes. "But I don't want another house! I mean, what does he think he's doing, leaving me that much money? It's yours. It should be yours. I'll give it back, that's what I'll do. Can I do that?"

Alex could only smile at her distress. "The money's not important to me, Stacey. If you don't want to buy a house, you can put it aside for Emily's education." He paused and glanced around the sterile room. The place was giving him claustrophobia. "Let's get out of here." He folded the document lengthwise and stuck it in his breast pocket.

Soon they were back in Alex's car, heading home. Neither of them said a word until he pulled up to the curb and cut the engine.

"I thought you'd just drop me off and go back to work," Stacey said. "What about your meeting?"

"It's over by now," he said as they both got out of the car. "Anyway, who wants to be cooped up in a meeting room on a fine summer morning like this?

Come on, Stacey, come sit with me on the porch swing. We still have a few decisions to make."

His invitation was full of warmth, and it filled her with hope. She allowed him to take her hand long enough to lead her to the porch. Seemingly in no hurry, he removed his jacket and draped it over the back of the newly painted swing, then sat down with a deceptively contented-sounding sigh.

Stacey hovered nearby, undeniably worried about what he might have up his sleeve, but made no move to sit beside him.

"This is a very interesting turn of events, wouldn't you say?" he asked. When she didn't answer, he continued. "Suddenly our roles are reversed. I'm the landlord and you're the tenant. How much rent do you think I ought to charge you? Or maybe I should just evict you."

For a moment she panicked, taking his words at face value. "Oh, Alex, please let Emily and me stay in the apartment. I know you don't need the rental income, but we've carved out a real home for ourselves here with you. Don't tear it apart. At least if we live here together we can work on our relationship—"

In one swift, sure lunge he grabbed her arm, pulled her down into his lap and silenced her with a kiss. His mouth worked against hers, first hard and insistent, then soft and teasing, until she melted against him in acquiescence. Here, at least, was one area in which their bodies, minds and souls were in complete agreement.

When he had kissed her as thoroughly as was possible in full view of the neighbors, he lifted his mouth from hers and gazed intently at her.

"You weren't serious," she said, stating the obvious.

He cupped her cheek in his hand. "Oh, I meant every word. You and Emily may *not* live in the attic apartment. Emily can have the bedroom with the rosebud wallpaper, where she used to stay before you moved upstairs. And you—you can share the master bedroom with me."

Her eyes widened in momentary shock.

"After we're married," he added quickly.

She squeezed her eyes shut, but when she opened them again he was still there, staring expectantly at her. "You mean that?" she asked.

"Yes. Stacey, I tried like hell not to fall in love with you. After I went and did it anyway, I thought that I could protect myself from the hurt of losing you, the way I lost Jeanne, by making damn sure nothing happened to you. But all I accomplished was to drive a wedge between us by trying to force you to live by my standards.

"Then yesterday morning, when I was packing up to leave, it hit me hard. I realized that if I lost you through my own bullheadedness, and you were gone from my life for good, it would hurt every bit as much as if you'd died."

"Oh, Alex." Her cheeks were wet with tears. "You won't lose me. And you can be as bullheaded as you want—I'll learn to deal with it. I might still show you my temper sometimes, and I might say things I don't mean—"

"I'll try not to take it so hard." He brushed her tears away with his thumb.

She smiled then. "I'll expect you to cook."

"You'll have to teach me how to make something besides meat loaf and beef stroganoff."

"And I doubt you'll ever convince me or Emily to wear shoes all the time in the summer."

"I can live with that. I'd like to adopt her, you know."

"Emily?" Her eyes filled again, then overflowed. "Oh, Alex, that'd be great. You'll make a wonderful dad." She slipped her arms around his neck and pulled him closer, absorbing the warmth of his body, the security of his strength.

"Is that a yes?" he asked.

"What was the question?"

"I never really asked it. Will you marry me?"

"You know I will."

They kissed again, a long, slow, lingering embrace that warmed Stacey from the inside out. She almost reeled from the happiness she'd found so unexpectedly, in the most unlikely place. And silently she thanked the ornery old man who had made it all happen.

By Tuesday evening Stacey and Alex had put the house back together, so that when Betty and Emily arrived from Kansas City it was impossible to tell that any packing had taken place.

Emily greeted her mother and her "Uncle Alex" with rampant enthusiasm, but as the adults settled in the living room, she quickly lost interest in their conversation and wandered upstairs to find her kitten.

"Mom, Alex and I have something to tell you—" Stacey began, but Betty immediately cut her off.

"You're getting married!"

Alex and Stacey looked at each other, bewildered. "How did you know?" Alex asked.

"Oh, phooey, any idiot could see how in love you two are. It was only a matter of time. Chester and I— I mean, Chester knew what he was doing."

Stacey rose from the sofa, hands on hips. "You were in cahoots with Chester all along! Mom, how could you so shamelessly manipulate your own daughter?"

Betty smiled serenely. "Are you sorry I did?"

Stacey smiled back. "No." Then she looked at Alex. "Let's tell Emily the news. At least we can surprise *her*."

"Nothing surprises that child," Betty observed.

"Do you think she'll understand what it means, that we're getting married?" Alex asked, his brow creased in concern.

"Maybe not, but she'll catch on to the concept of a new daddy."

He beamed at that.

Emily was at that moment making her way down the curved staircase. At Stacey's summons she scampered into the living room. "George missed me," she announced.

"I'm sure he did," Stacey said, scooping Emily into her lap. "We have something to tell you. Alex and I are going to be married. Do you know what that means?"

Emily nodded solemnly.

Stacey wasn't convinced. "We're going to be a family," she persisted. "Alex is going to be your dad."

The little girl nodded again. "I know."

"You *know?*" Stacey threw an accusing glance at her mother, but Betty only shrugged innocently. "How did you know that, pumpkin?"

"Chester told me," Emily announced before squirming down from Stacey's lap and dashing off again.

* * * * *

NORA ROBERTS

Love has a language all its own, and for centuries, flowers have symbolized love's finest expression. Discover the language of flowers—and love—in this romantic collection of 48 favorite books by bestselling author Nora Roberts.

Starting in February, two titles will be available each month at your favorite retail outlet.

In February, look for:

Irish Thoroughbred, **Volume #1**
The Law Is A Lady, **Volume #2**

In March, look for:

Irish Rose, **Volume #3**
Storm Warning, **Volume #4**

Collect all 48 titles and become fluent in

THE LANGUAGE of LOVE

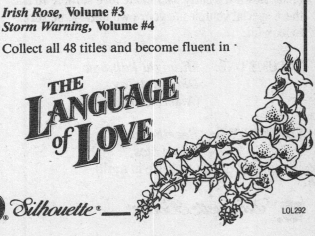

Silhouette®

LOL292

From the popular author of the bestselling title
DUNCAN'S BRIDE (Intimate Moments #349)
comes the

LINDA HOWARD COLLECTION

Two exquisite collector's editions that contain four of
Linda Howard's early passionate love stories. To add
these special volumes to your own library, be sure
to look for:

VOLUME ONE: *Midnight Rainbow*
Diamond Bay
(Available in March)

VOLUME TWO: *Heartbreaker*
White Lies
(Available in April)

SLH92

Take 4 bestselling love stories FREE

Plus get a FREE surprise gift!

Special Limited-time Offer

Mail to Silhouette Reader Service™

In the U.S.	In Canada
3010 Walden Avenue	P.O. Box 609
P.O. Box 1867	Fort Erie, Ontario
Buffalo, N.Y. 14269-1867	L2A 5X3

YES! Please send me 4 free Silhouette Romance® novels and my free surprise gift. Then send me 6 brand-new novels every month, which I will receive months before they appear in bookstores. Bill me at the low price of $2.25* each—a savings of 34¢ apiece off cover prices. There are no shipping, handling or other hidden costs. I understand that accepting the books and gift places me under no obligation ever to buy any books. I can always return a shipment and cancel at any time. Even if I never buy another book from Silhouette, the 4 free books and the surprise gift are mine to keep forever.

*Offer slightly different in Canada—$2.25 per book plus 69¢ per shipment for delivery. Canadian residents add applicable federal and provincial sales tax. Sales tax applicable in N.Y.

215 BPA ADL9   315 BPA ADMN

Name _____ (PLEASE PRINT) _____

Address _____ Apt. No. _____

City _____ State/Prov. _____ Zip/Postal Code _____

This offer is limited to one order per household and not valid to present Silhouette Romance® subscribers. Terms and prices are subject to change.

SROM-91   © 1990 Harlequin Enterprises Limited

WHEN A PISCES MAN MEETS A PISCES WOMAN...

Normally cool, calm and collected Pisces man David Waterman had never felt quite so hot-blooded! David didn't know why fellow Piscean Eugenia "Storky" Jones had "bought" him at a charity auction, but he planned on finding out—fast. Discover the delightful truth in March's STORKY JONES IS BACK IN TOWN by Anne Peters—only from Silhouette Romance. It's WRITTEN IN THE STARS!

Available in March at your favorite retail outlet, or order your copy now by sending your name, address, zip or postal code, along with a check or money order for $2.69 (please do not send cash), plus 75¢ postage and handling ($1.00 in Canada), payable to Silhouette Reader Service to:

In the U.S.
3010 Walden Ave.
P.O. Box 1396
Buffalo, NY 14269-1396

In Canada
P.O. Box 609
Fort Erie, Ontario
L2A 5X3

Please specify book title with your order.
Canadian residents add applicable federal and provincial taxes.

SR392R